He watched the bar owner move off as Fontana touched his shoulder. "What the hell were you doing up there anyway, Jack? What kind of job did you take that left you standing guard over a dead Chinaman?"

Cleary rubbed the back of his neck where a painful stiffness was demanding attention. "The guy had jumped bail on some penny-ante grocery theft. I was hired to bring him in, save the bondsman two hundred bucks," he finished bitterly.

"I wondered what your excuse for coming back was, Jack," said Fontana, his face sober. "I remember that case. It's not worth the court costs. If you hadn't taken the job, the bail bondsman would have written off his loss next week, and forgotten it by the week after that."

"The poor Chinese got written off instead," said Cleary, feeling his features tighten.

"I don't know why you're giving yourself such a rash about one lousy Chinaman, Cleary," said Hine licking sauce off his fingers.

"The man's dead, Hine. Somebody shot him. Doesn't that mean anything to you?"

Sfakis leaned around his partner to look down the bar at Cleary. "You ain't been down here in a while, Cleary. Maybe you forgot. Nobody dies in Chinatown."

PRIVATE EYE #4
NOBODY DIES IN CHINATOWN

A novel by
MAX LOCKHART

Based on the Universal Television Series **PRIVATE EYE**
Created by Anthony Yerkovich

Adapted from the episodes
"Nobody Dies in Chinatown" teleplay by John Leekley &
Alfonse Ruggiero, Jr., story by Anthony Yerkovich &
John Leekley & Alfonse Ruggiero, Jr., and "War Buddy"
teleplay by Alfonse Ruggiero, Jr., story by Anthony
Yerkovich & John Leekley & Alfonse Ruggiero, Jr.

IVY BOOKS • NEW YORK

Ivy Books
Published by Ballantine Books
Copyright © 1988 by MCA Publishing Rights, a Division of
MCA Inc. All rights reserved.

Library of Congress Catalog Card Number: 87-92091

ISBN 0-8041-0272-4

Manufactured in the United States of America

First Edition: May 1988

P R O L O G U E

Onstage at The Crescendo Club black satin gowns on black satin skin shimmered in the oval of hot white light as Mary Hart and the Van Horns belted out the rock and roll strains of "He'll Be Back" to the late-night crowd of Sunset Strip hipsters.

> . . . he goes, but that's okay
> 'Cause he'll be back. Don't ask me
> How I know . . . He'll be back . . .
> He can sail the seven seas
> I don't have to keep track . . .
> 'Cause he'll be back.

Backstage at The Crescendo Club, dust motes floated in the shadows cast by the dim light as Eddie Parris belted out the rhythm and blues of the cuckolded male. Transplanted Trenton, New Jersey, would-be rock and roll impresario variety.

"She's trying to kill me!" screamed Eddie Parris as he rolled his eyes and grabbed the back curtain, balling it up in one fist like a baby with a blanket. "She's trying to kill me!" he repeated for dramatic effect, staggering back and collapsing on a stool. Unfortunately he failed to let go of the curtain.

With only mild interest, Jack Cleary watched the corner of the curtain tear away from its moorings, listened to the Van Horns crank the volume up another fifty decibels to cover the sound of ripping cloth, and then focused his weary eyes on his twitching client, all five feet, three inches of him.

"Take it easy, Eddie," he said, without any real hope that Eddie would. His kind never did. They lived on dreams and Scotch, and too damn much of both. Like private detectives, thought Cleary wryly.

Eddie Parris studied the half-dozen 8 by 10s and bit the backstage curtain. After chewing madly, his eyes flickering from photo to photo, he spat out the soggy mass and looked up at Cleary. "She never did that with me," he said in a plaintive voice.

After comparing the well-muscled, nude male body in the photos to Eddie's scrawny frame, Cleary could understand why. He shrugged his shoulders. He wasn't paid to make smart-ass comments.

Eddie unwrapped a roll of Tums, crunched into a handful, and washed them down with most of his double Scotch. He stabbed at the photos with one finger. "Do you have any more of these?"

"My man took four rolls before he ran out of film."

He wondered why Eddie wanted more. Jesus, the ones he had covered most of the positions in the *Kama Sutra*. So far as he knew, the couple in the surveillance photos had tried them all.

Eddie picked up an 8 by 10 and studied it, his pinched face turning tight and red. "*Four rolls!* The lousy, two-timing bitch!"

"Want some free advice, Eddie?" asked Cleary, then winced as the singer turned a hopeful face toward him. Why the hell did clients always think he had all the answers? He hadn't even figured out the questions yet. "Get rid of her. She's ruining your life."

Eddie slumped down further on his stool, sadly shaking his head. He looked up hopefully at the band's manager. "What do you think?"

The manager moved closer, trying to peer at the photos. "The man ain't woofen, Eddie. It's the fourth time since we left Atlantic City."

"Pittsburgh doesn't count!" retorted Eddie, jerking the pictures out of the manager's lascivious visual range.

Jack Cleary shrugged his shoulders again and moved off. There was nothing more he could do here. Eddie had paid his money and taken his chance. He would go on being a doormat to his wife, a ripe nineteen-year-old package of talent and raw sexuality who had already been opened and sampled, evidently by anybody who could undo her wrapping.

Cleary hesitated as he stepped through the door from the backstage area. Maybe he ought to say something else. Then he glanced toward the stage and Mary Hart's gyrating pelvis, thought of the pelvis in the photographs, and discarded the idea. He would buy Eddie a bottle of Scotch and another package of Tums instead.

He dropped onto a bar stool with the weariness of thirty-six years of life and twice that of experience. He glanced in the mirror behind the bar and noticed his eyes looked more red than blue, and the stubble on his chin reminded him he hadn't shaved within the last twenty-four hours. Maybe longer than that. He didn't remember. He rubbed his chin and considered his reflection. His wasn't a bad face, given the amount of mileage on it. A few lines around the eyes, a sharpness to the cheekbones, a certain stiffness about the mouth that said he didn't smile much. Did he look like a private eye, or an ex-cop? He studied the face in the mirror. Both, he guessed. And why not? He was both. Thrown out of the LAPD on a trumped-up bribery charge, he had taken over his brother's detective agency after Nick was murdered. He was a private eye by choice.

He grinned to himself. Choice, hell. Who was he kidding? He was a gumshoe private dick because that's all he could be. How else could he pack an iron and fight for truth, justice, and the American way? He sobered and beckoned to the bartender.

"Yeah, Cleary," said the bartender, wiping his hands on the tail end of a towel. "Want the usual?"

"Sure," said Cleary, glancing back at the stage.

"Wouldn't mind a piece of that," said the bartender, pouring him a shot of I.W. Harper.

"You and a lot of other people," said Jack cynically, thinking that little Mary Hart had come a long way from her daddy's gospel choir in Salem, South Carolina. He lifted his glass. "Welcome to the Strip, Mary Hart," he whispered. "Street of broken dreams and cheap Scotch." He drank and set his glass down. "And private eyes who hide in closets to take dirty pictures and talk to themselves about choices."

He glanced down the bar and watched the bartender pass a bottle over half a dozen shot glasses in a row, sloshing liquor on the bar. Over the screaming decibels of Mary Hart and the Van Horns he heard a deep voice.

"...you got to understand, I was blind drunk on mescal. The damn horse was smarter than I was. He pulled up and I went ass over teakettle, right past the cameras and into the gorge. Broke a leg, busted some ribs, cracked my collarbone, rearranged my nose. If I hadn't been so fucking drunk, I'd really been hurt."

Cleary slid off his stool and started down the bar, feeling a grin pull at his mouth.

Joe Quinlan interrupted his story to pick up a drink from the row of shot glasses and hold it up in a toast. "Here's to smart horses and dumb stuntmen."

Everybody followed his lead, and Joe snatched the bottle from Scotty, the bartender, and refilled the shot glasses, sloshing still more liquor on the bar. He slammed the bottle down and turned back to his circle of admirers, his eyes sparkling with the recklessness of the born troublemaker.

"This pretty little brown orderly smuggled me out of the hospital, got me started cliff diving after the bandages came off. She took all my money and left me in Acapulco with a busted eardrum and six hundred dollars in bar bills—"

"And two hundred worth of bail which you still owe me for," Cleary broke in.

"Son of a gun!" said Joe, his face breaking into a huge crooked grin.

"What do you say, Joe?" asked Cleary, grinning back at him.

"Well, if you aren't a sight for sore eyes!" exclaimed Joe, clamping a paw around Cleary's shoulders, the thick plaster cast on his forearm making Cleary feel as though he were being hugged by Popeye.

Cleary examined his friend and decided the years were showing. A broken nose that mended in a bump, reddish-brown hair creeping up his forehead, lines around the eyes and mouth, and dressed in a seedy-looking brown-figured shirt and cheap plaid jacket, Joe Quinlan looked as if he was on the down-hill side of an ill-spent life. Considering he and Joe were the same age, Cleary decided his own face was holding its own.

"Hey, Quinlan, you told me to boot you out of here by ten," said Scotty, tapping Joe on the shoulder.

"You got to be somewhere?" asked Cleary, thumping him in the chest with his elbow.

Joe glanced at his watch, a frown marking his rugged features, then the reckless grin reappeared. "Nothing that can't wait. Scotty, a couple of shots for me and my old buddy, John Francis Cleary."

Joe dumped a wad of money on the bar, and Cleary watched a dime slide across the polished wood. What the hell, he thought. He didn't have anything better to do except chase down a Chinese who had jumped bail. And he didn't choose to go to Chinatown tonight. A man still had choices.

He lifted a shot glass. Behind him he heard Mary Hart belting out another stanza, felt the beat pounding against his eardrums.

> He'll be back... Don't ask me
> How I know. Got no special secret.
> No expensive French perfumes.
> But I know he'll never leave me
> Once I get him in my room.

"To choices," he said aloud, and tossed down his drink.

As he stood outside The Crescendo Club a few hours later, Cleary decided he had been drunker. A lot drunker. He was still able to stand without a tilt, still able to put his hand in his pocket at the first attempt, still able to find his valet ticket without turning his pocket inside out. Life was improving.

"Hey, Joe. Good luck against the Indians Saturday night," Scotty called through the open door.

Joe emptied a glass and tossed it back in the club. "Put a few bucks on the Thunderbolts. We're gonna scalp the Indians."

"Let's see, since the last time I saw you, you've been a bull rider, stuntman, cliff diver. Now it's Roller Derby," said Cleary, eyeing Joe's alcohol-flushed face.

Joe nodded, the neon lights striping his face with black-and-white bars. "Sport of the future. More Roller Derby ovals being built every day. We're gonna end up with our pictures on bubble gum cards just like baseball players." He reached in his pocket and pulled out two tickets. "Here you go. A couple of ringside seats."

"When the hell are you going to slow down?"

"When they nail the coffin shut. Come on. We get a move on and we can catch a nightcap up the street." He searched his pockets. "Looks like you're going to have to spot me a couple rounds. I blew my whole wad in that dump."

He had a sheepish look on his face that Cleary recognized. You always had to spot Joe a couple, he thought as he handed his ticket to the valet. Money ran through his fingers like water through a sieve. If it weren't for Eileen Quinlan standing around with a bucket to catch the leaks, Joe would be flat busted most of the time.

"So how are you and Eileen doing these days?" he asked, turning around to find the ex-stuntman had quietly disappeared. "Hey, Joe?" he called, looking up and down the street and finally spotting him ducking behind the broad beam of a '55 Lincoln. "You lose something?"

Joe put his finger to his lips, his eyes glittering with enjoyment. "Do you see three no-necks in a black New Yorker going up the street?"

"Yeah, but they're not going up the street any-more," said Cleary as the gleaming front end of the '55 New Yorker plowed over the curb and slammed to a halt in front of him.

Joe, his eyes mirroring the potential explosiveness of a Molotov cocktail in the hands of a Hungarian freedom fighter, straightened up as two huge leg-breakers, led by Sidney Bloom, erupted out of the black car like steam out of a geyser, but considerably more substantial.

"You with me on this, Jack?" he asked, his eyes never leaving the three muscle-bound hoods.

"Do I have a choice?" asked Cleary, sighing and flexing his hand in preparation for a few rounds. He had forgotten another problem of being Joe Quinlan's buddy. Sooner or later you were going to get involved in a fight, because Joe collected trouble about as fast as he spent money. This time it looked as if Jack Cleary, private eye, had a good chance of getting the shit kicked out of him.

"With these guys? I doubt it," replied Joe, cocking his fists.

"I hate these situations," said Cleary, tossing away his cigarette.

"We been looking all over the Strip for you, Quinlan," said Bloom, flexing huge biceps and grinning in anticipation.

Joe grinned back as he suddenly threw his jacket over Bloom's head. "You found me," he said as he delivered a perfect punch with his good hand.

Legbreakers One and Two seemed to resent the sight of their boss sitting on his rear in the gutter, and went to work with fists and feet on Joe. Cleary admired their economy of motion. It was always a pleasure to watch professionals at work. However...

He grabbed Legbreaker Two, spun him around, and decked him. "Two against one isn't fair, punk."

"So you want to play?" asked Legbreaker Two, bouncing back to his feet and smashing Cleary in the face.

Cleary, reeling backward, tasted his own blood and decided he didn't like the coppery flavor. If he was going to play Count Dracula, he would open up someone else's veins. "Hey, son of a bitch!" he shouted at Legbreaker Two.

Son of a bitch turned back and bumped his chin on Cleary's fist. The results were so satisfactory that Cleary put his fist in the way of the hood's nose, and waited until proboscis met knuckles. "Legs a little wobbly, punk? Ready for a little nap?" he asked as he whirled the man around, grabbed a fistful of jacket, and ran him into the front grille of a parked car.

"Sleep tight, and don't let the bedbugs bite," said Cleary as he stepped around the thug.

In the meantime, Legbreaker One had discovered that fists were no defense against a plaster cast across the forehead, not to mention the back of the skull, the shoulders, the chest, and the belly.

"You got a dirty nose," said Quinlan. "Better wipe

it." He aided the hood by dropping him like a sack of potatoes and substituting asphalt for a handkerchief. Legbreaker One lost interest in the proceedings as he lay facedown, with bits of plaster floating down on his body like dandruff on a black suit.

"Bastard!" screamed Bloom, emerging from underneath Joe's coat and trying to scramble to his feet and go for his gun.

"Excuse me," said Cleary politely, shoving a wingtip through Bloom's lung cavity. "I didn't see you down there." He gestured to Joe, and they strolled with giant steps toward Cleary's Eldorado, delivered by the valet who'd long since disappeared to safety inside The Crescendo.

"Just like old times, huh?" asked Joe.

Cleary glanced back at the three peacefully snoozing thugs. Correction, he thought. Two snoozing thugs, and one retching in the gutter. "You mind telling me what that was all about?"

"Just some guys I was supposed to meet."

Cleary gave him the same kind of look he used to give robbery suspects he had caught coming out of a liquor store with nylon stockings over their faces.

"You know, some debt-collecting guys that were sent," said Joe, wiggling like a kid caught with his hand in the cookie jar.

Cleary opened the Eldorado door. "Sent? Sent by who?"

Joe wiggled some more, glanced back down the street, then finally answered. "Ever heard of a guy called Mickey Gold?"

Cleary wiped his mouth, considered the blood smeared on his hand, and wondered if he had better develop a taste for it. "Joseph, are you telling me we just beat the hell out of three legbreakers that belong to the biggest mobster in L.A.?"

"It's good to see you, Jack," said Quinlan, a guilty grin on his face as they both slid into the Eldorado.

"Shit," said Cleary, and decided to lay in a supply of Tums and Scotch.

PRINCIPLE OF BLAH BLAH

O N E

Cleary parked his Eldorado in front of Mickey Gold's Black and Tan Club, a stucco building that boasted a covered walk bounded by a waist-high wall topped by fluted arches. Marble urns containing some unidentifiable shrub sat in the exact center of each arch. Mickey Gold claimed the building had class. Cleary thought it looked like the set for some low-budget French foreign legion movie. He always expected some burnoose-clad, would-be Errol Flynn with camel dung on his boots to leap from one of the arches and run down the Strip with a drawn sword.

Cleary slid out of his car. Slowly. Feeling every one of his thirty-six years. Plus twenty. He slammed the door and winced as the sound reverberated through his skull. He caught sight of his reflection in the car's gleaming finish and winced again. Between the residual effects of a night on the town with Joe Quinlan and severe knuckle impact, he looked like something the street cleaners had scraped out of the gutter.

Ambling stiffly over to the glass display case, he checked out the photos of Nick Roma, the headliner for the Black and Tan Club. He had a choice. He could skip Nick Roma. He wished he could skip Mickey Gold, too, but he owed Joe Quinlan. He owed a lot of debts, he thought. Some he couldn't pay— images of the delicate feaures of a dead Chinese girl flickered at the edges of his mind. But maybe his debt to Joe was payable. He hoped so, he thought as he entered the Black and Tan Club. Because the very sound of Mickey Gold's voice gave him a headache.

He hesitated in the doorway and surveyed the club. Sidney Bloom, the leader in last night's fight, stood behind the bar using a funnel to pour cheap liquor into bottles with expensive labels. Cleary made a mental note not to buy a drink in the Black and Tan. He also noted that Bloom's sunglasses didn't do much to hide the bruises. The sight of those bruises improved Cleary's headache almost as much as aspirin.

Reluctantly Cleary shifted his attention to Meyer Alliance, Mickey Gold's money man. He didn't particularly enjoy looking at Meyer, but it beat looking at the sleazy accountant's boss. Meyer was sitting at Mickey's table, which served as office, dining room, and for all the Strip knew, Gold's bedroom.

A phone sprouted out of Meyer's ear. "I'm not sure that's what we have in mind," he said as his eyes swiveled toward the man himself.

"Don't whine, Meyer," said Gold. "Just tell him the terms."

Cleary wished he had chewed a handful of Tums. If the sound of Mickey Gold's voice gave him a headache, the sight of Mickey Gold gave him a bellyache.

Mickey Gold was a sawed-off barrel of a man whose slightly bulging eyes always reminded Cleary of an evil Peter Lorre. An ex-pug who had fought his way out of the slums using his fists, his brains, and much as Cleary hated to admit it, his moxie, Gold was always fastidiously barbered and tailored, and wrapped in a fog of cologne and talcum powder. A pudgy man who gave the impression of being fatter than he was, his vitality seemed to fill the room like a noxious smog as he paced about in a green satin smoking jacket. A tailor with a mouthful of pins duckwalked after him in a futile effort to fit the mobster for a pair of slacks.

"You call this sharkskin?" Mickey asked the tailor, pointing to a swatch of material. "We don't call this sharkskin where I come from."

The tailor just nodded, a look of resignation in his eyes. Cleary could think of at least a dozen places on Mickey's anatomy where he wished the tailor would stick his pins. But then Mickey would stomp the tailor into a grease spot, and Cleary didn't wish the man ill. The poor guy was just trying to make a living.

Mickey Gold turned to Meyer. "Tell the bloodsucker fifteen grand and we'll cut him a percentage. A small one," he added under his breath.

"I'm sure we can go as high as fifteen thousand, and we'll take care of you out of our end," Meyer translated.

"Hang up, Meyer."

"Got to go," said Meyer obediently.

Mickey pulled his pant leg away from the tailor and grabbed a piece of cake off a nearby dessert cart.

"Borrow money, you got to pay it back, Cleary." He slid into a booth with tufted gold velvet seats. "Why does a smart guy like you want to get mixed up with a *shnorer* like that?"

Cleary shrugged his shoulders. He might have known that Mickey saw him the minute he walked into the Black and Tan. He also should have guessed the mobster would have known who busted up his legbreakers. When it came to trouble on his turf, Mickey Gold had eyes in the front, back, and sides of his head.

"Take a walk," Mickey said to the tailor. "And I need that suit no later than six o'clock tonight."

The frustrated tailor looked for a moment as if he could sink a pin into Mickey's ample rump, but instinct for survival stopped him. Cleary sympathized. Survival influenced a lot of men's choices.

Mickey forked a big slice of cake into his mouth, masticated like a mean-eyed bull, then gestured to the waiter. "Oooo, this is wonderful. What is it, chocolate caramel swirl?" He turned to Cleary. "You want some?"

Cleary mostly wanted Mickey to stop talking with his mouth full. It didn't help his bellyache. "I want Quinlan off the hook, Gold."

"Off the hook? I'm not running a charitable organization here. I'm a businessman." He acted insulted at the very idea, but with an audible sigh like a put-upon executive, turned to Meyer. "What's this guy owe?"

Meyer turned to a page in a ledger. "Borrowed two thousand on the first of last month"—ran his finger across the page to another column—"no payments."

"Always has a song and dance," interjected Sidney from the bar. Cleary noticed the legbreaker's voice sounded weak. Must be having trouble with his chest. A leather-soled wingtip did that to a man.

"Owes four thousand five hundred as of last night, with the interest compounded daily," continued Meyer in his dryest accountant's voice. Cleary figured Meyer was out of place. He ought to be a banker specializing in throwing widows and orphans out of their homes.

"Twenty-five hundred in vig on a two-thousand-dollar loan?" asked Cleary.

Mickey looked offended again. "It's business."

"Come on, Mickey. Quinlan's no tourist. Let's work something out."

The mobster ignored him, and Cleary felt a rage begin to build like steam in an unvented engine. "I can still make a lot of trouble for you, Gold, badge or no badge."

Mickey picked through cloth swatches on his table, but Cleary knew the mobster had heard him and was merely buying time.

Mickey held up a cloth swatch. "Does this look like eggshell to you?" he asked Meyer.

"I'm out of patience, Gold," said Cleary. "Do we deal, or do I kick your teeth out at the earliest opportunity?"

"What is this Quinlan guy to you anyway?" asked Mickey.

"I operate on a need-to-know basis, and you don't need to know," replied Cleary. Gold was going to deal, his gut instinct told him so. He leaned over the table and pointed to the eggshell-colored swatch. "Don't pick that color. It wouldn't flatter you."

Skates flashed across the slanted wood oval at a tremendous rate of speed. A loud grunt and a body hit the wood, ass first, knocking the wind out of the bouncing figure as he slid down the embankment. Cleary dismissed the figure with a sympathetic wince of pain and focused instead on the padded, bandaged, taped-together, beaten-up gladiator body of Joe Quinlan. Cleary wondered how much longer Joe's body would hold together.

Head down, digging in, skating far ahead of the other skaters, intent, in his element, clearly enjoying the raw speed, Joe bore down on a pack of skaters slashing across the oval. Clasping hands with a huge, ponytailed Thunderbolt defense man who catapulted him forward as two Indians, muscled up and taped like defensive linemen, fell back like two pit bulls waiting to disembowel him. Or at least break something vital, like both legs and his head.

Joe speed-skated to the top of the oval, hung there like an ominous beast of prey, and then suddenly swooped down at forty mph, dipped inside on one wild-swinging Indian defensive man, then popped up and leveled him with a tomahawk chop of his padded cast. Cleary decided Roller Derby and street fighting had a lot in common.

Two Indian defense men caught Joe in a vise, both whaling away at him as they skated, knocking his helmet flying. With a wild war cry of his own that Custer would have recognized, Joe threw back both arms and sent the two Indians crashing back in tandem. Speeding toward the last two Indians, he darted left and then right, came up behind them, and hip checked one into the infield. With a lightening fast move, he bashed the other Indian with a head butt, sending him flying into the rail with a bone-rattling thud. Cleary figured Custer could've used Joe Quinlan.

Joe did a three-hundred-sixty-degree turnaround on the rail in front of Cleary and skated around the oval with his arms raised in victory as the announcer gave the score.

> And it's all tied at ten to ten
> at the end of the first period.
> Let's hear it for Wild Man, Joe Quinlan!

"That's your buddy?" asked Johnny Betts as he watched Joe skate into the infield.

Cleary nodded, amused by Johnny's wild-eyed look.

"What do ya feed him? Raw meat and gun powder? I seen alligators down in the Louisiana swamps that look friendlier than him."

"Funny you should mention that," said Cleary, lighting a cigarette. "Joe used to wrestle alligators down and eat them raw, then have a rock and roll singer for dessert."

Johnny's eyes were a little rounder. "You're kiddin' me. Aren't ya?"

Cleary took a drag off his cigarette. "Yeah, kid. He just broke the singer's arms."

Johnny opened his mouth to retort, but the announcer interrupted.

> Hold on to your hats, ladies and gentlemen,
> get ready for the little ladies.

Johnny smoothed down his Brylcreemed, gravity-defying pompadour. "Little ladies, huh? I think I'll stick around for this."

Cleary grinned. "Turn around and say hello to the 'little' ladies, Betts."

Johnny turned, and Cleary shifted to one side to watch the younger man's face. He wouldn't miss seeing this for a night with Marilyn Monroe. Well, maybe he would. But Marilyn was busy tonight. "My, what big eyes you have, Grandma," he said to Betts.

Johnny's mouth was gaping open as he looked at the flaming redhead and the Blond Bombshell standing next to him, waiting their turn to go on. With their helmets, padded uniforms, and roller skates, both Amazons towered over him. Cleary managed to swallow back his laughter as Johnny's eyes bulged out of his head when the blonde adjusted her size D cups with both hands.

The redhead caught Johnny staring like a fish with a goiter and elbowed her partner. "Hey, you got a spectator."

The blonde glared at Johnny from icicle-blue eyes. "Hey! Whatta you looking at?"

Johnny swallowed, then vapor locked.

"My friend here's a big fan of yours," said Cleary.

"Oh, yeah?" asked the blonde, checking Johnny out with a head-to-toe look that stripped him down to his jockstrap. Or maybe less. She liked what she saw. "Then maybe you ought to stop around after the match, doll face." She squared her shoulders and stuck her chest out like the prow of the *Queen Mary*.

Cleary decided Johnny needed a few lessons on how to keep a poker face. His expression said plainly that bullmastiffs and Chihuahuas were mismatched. The young man finally managed a choked smile. "Thanks, uh, I'd really like that, but"—he cast Cleary a frantic glance that Cleary pretended not to see—"the fact is I'm kinda previously occupied work-wise for my boss here."

Johnny smiled desperately in Cleary's direction. Cleary ground out his cigarette under his heel and clapped Johnny on the back in his best Dutch-uncle fashion. "I've never been one to stand in the way of young love, kid." He pasted a benevolent, ball-busting grin on his face. "Hell, take the whole night off."

The blonde snapped on her chin strap. "Well, now that *that's* settled—"

The redhead interrupted her with an elbow. "There's Blanche Weston . . ."

The blonde's expression turned murderous, and Johnny's turned desperate. "Let's kill that bitch," she said to her partner.

She glanced down at Johnny and her expression did a hundred-and-eighty-degree turn to coquettish. "I'll be looking for ya, sugar." She waggled her finger, then she and the redhead rocketed off, fangs bared for Blanche Weston's blood.

Cleary figured if he were iron ore, Johnny's look would smelt him. "That was mean-spirited," said Johnny between gritted teeth.

Cleary shrugged and pushed the young street hustler in the direction of the locker room. "Think of it as a challenge, kid. See if you can rise to the occasion."

"Hey, man, she'd swallow me whole."

Cleary weighed Johnny's words against his expression, choked back his comments, and then pushed open the locker room door and walked past Thunderbolts sprawled out on the benches in the drab room of institutional green walls and battered lockers. Cleary breathed in the tart scent of analgesic, the acrid smell of cigarette smoke as players lit up, the sour odor of beer as cans were punched open and passed around. Permeating the room, overlaying all the other odors, infiltrating the air, was the musky smell of sweating male bodies.

And what bodies they were: ex-pro-football players, boxers past their prime, men paid to give and take beatings, scarred veterans of a lifetime of contact sports. Each one was dealing with pain in his own way. Some adjusted tape on knees, wrists, elbows, ankles. Others checked equipment in a futile effort to pad their battered bodies against that one hospitalizing blow. A few just lay back gazing at the ceiling. Cleary instinctively knew those were the ones who were looking into the future. And not seeing one.

Johnny checked out the human wrecks washed up on the benches like flotsam on the beach, and shook his head. "Why do they do it?"

"It's all they know, kid," answered Cleary, looking around for Joe. He saw him gazing into the mirror over a chipped sink and bandaging his cut chin.

Slapping the bandage haphazardly in place, Joe grabbed a whiskey bottle out of a passing player's mouth and took a long pull. He looked around, a sneer curling up his lip. "You look like a bunch of godforsaken losers. C'mon. Let's give them a show. We can skate circles around these bums." He took another pull of whiskey and wiped his lips, sneering again as the players refused to meet his eyes.

"Hairy-assed pansies," he muttered as he skated over to Cleary and Johnny, slapping repeatedly at his bandage as it repeatedly peeled off. "These slobs from upstate always go for the cheap shots. They can't deck Joe Quinlan by cloutin' him in the chin." He grinned at Cleary. "What did you think of the game?"

Cleary ignored Joe's smile. "I talked to Mickey Gold."

"Gold? What'd you have to do that for?" he asked, shuffling his feet like a kid asking his mother why she talked to his math teacher without telling him first.

Cleary lost patience. "Damn it, Joe, I'm trying to keep your ass out of a sling."

"I never asked you to."

"It's a habit. I'll try to break it. In the meantime, we're going to meet Gold at The Crescendo at midnight tonight. He's dropping the vig. All you gotta do is pay fifty a week and everything is squared. And it might be a good idea if you buy his bodyguards a drink as kind of an apology."

Joe looked puzzled. "Apology? What for?"

Cleary mentally counted to ten. With a profane expression between every number. "Well, for rubbing one guy's face in the pavement. Braining another with that plaster of paris club of yours."

Joe grinned and waved his cast in the air. "Yeah, it really put his lights out."

"Joe," said Cleary, his teeth beginning to ache from being clenched together.

"You shouldn't have gone out on a limb for me, Jack."

"I already did. A long time ago," he added softly as the Thunderbolts skated noisily out of the locker room.

"Hey, Joe, come on," one of them called.

"I gotta go," said Quinlan, putting his helmet on.

"Midnight, okay, Joe?" asked Cleary, holding his gaze for a meaningful half beat.

Joe raised his hand and blasted outside, adjusting his pads as he left. The announcer's voice filled the empty locker room.

> Look out! There's Rosey McGuire
> and the Blond Bombshell pummeling
> Blanche Weston to a pulp.

"Mind if we go out the back way?" asked Johnny, his face a shade paler than a minute ago.

T W O

Cleary stood at the bar feeling like Prince Charming when Cinderella didn't show up in her glass slippers. In fact, The Crescendo Club reminded him of a ballroom that the fairy godmother skipped. The guests were gone, Scotty was stacking chairs on the tables, another bartender was polishing glasses with a dirty dishrag. Soon everybody would turn into mice and lizards and scurry back to whatever traps and watering cans they had been hiding in before a magic wand transformed them. Except for the rat. Mickey Gold was holding court for a young starlet draped in an apricot chiffon dress that did nothing for her modesty. Judging from the ripeness of her upper structure, Cleary decided she was playing the pumpkin.

Mickey talked and waved his arms, his plump cheeks jiggling, while a bruised Sidney Bloom hovered nearby. Cleary nodded to himself. All Mickey Gold needed were long whiskers sticking out by each corner of his mouth to look just like a rat. He watched Gold point to the dessert cart, and Sidney handed the mobster another cherries jubilee. Gold started shoveling the dessert in his mouth in between sentences, and Cleary wanted to gag. At least a rat kept his mouth shut when eating.

"... now it cost close to fifty Gs to have it bullet proofed. Used half-inch steel—that'll stop a bazooka—and the Beverly Hills cops won't let me drive it 'cause it's too heavy for the roads..." He stopped to take a bite, suddenly realized what he was doing, and pushed the half-eaten cherries jubilee away. "Damn it, Sidney, I told you I'm on a diet."

"Sorry, boss," mumbled Sidney. His voice still sounded odd, and Cleary wondered if he hadn't managed to unstick his lungs from his backbone yet.

Mickey glanced at his watch, then at Cleary, a satisfied look in his eyes. "We had a deal, Cleary. A very generous deal I wouldn't make with just anybody. But your buddy's not going to show, so now we do it my way."

Cleary let him get halfway up before speaking. No good reason except he wanted to see if the mobster needed a hoist. "Keep your shirt on, Gold. He'll be here."

"Yeah," said Joe, entering the bar with a fresh bandage on his chin, face flushed with drink, and the afterglow of competition in the form of fresh bruises. "Where's the fire, Mickey?" He saw the young starlet and grinned. "Your pants hot or something?"

Ignoring Mickey's rapidly purpling face, he walked

over to Cleary. "Sorry I'm late, Jack. Martinez broke his femur in three places so we had to run him over to St. Paul's." He shook his head like a husband explaining why he was three hours late for dinner. "I had to help him kill off a fifth of bourbon before he'd let 'em set it."

Cleary could believe it. Joe's breath had enough alcohol on it to catch fire if you held a match in front of his mouth.

"Where the hell's my money, Quinlan?" demanded Mickey, his nose twitching. Just like a rat's, thought Cleary.

"Relax, will ya? I'm talking to my friend." Joe snatched the bottle of champagne out of the cooler and poured himself a glass. He dumped a handful of crumpled bills on the zebra-striped tabletop. A couple of coins scattered across the wood. "What say we all have a drink," he continued in the cheerful voice of a Boy Scout at a wiener roast.

"Get the money, Sidney," commanded Mickey.

"Help yourself," said Joe, sipping his champagne as Sidney counted the crumpled bills.

"All he's got is eleven bucks," said Sidney in disbelief.

Joe leaned closer to Cleary, who wished he hadn't. "I had to front Martinez some dough for the hospital bill."

Mickey's face began to swell. "You come to me with eleven lousy dollars..."

Joe touched the coins on the table. "And sixty-two cents. Nearly two-thirds of a dollar. Don't get your bowels in an uproar. I'll pay you next week."

Mickey's eyes burned as if a fire were smoldering somewhere in their mean depths. "There ain't going to be any next week, you broken-down has-been. Sidney, check his pockets. Bastard's probably holding out on us."

"I'll front him the rest, Gold," said Cleary quickly, smelling more than alcohol and Mickey's cologne in the air. There was the metallic odor of violence, like the air before a thunderstorm.

Sidney reached into Joe's inside jacket pocket, and Joe pushed him away, his face revealing suppressed rage aggravated by alcohol. "I don't think you want to do that," he said to Sidney. He gave Cleary a sideways glance. "I'm trying to be nice, Jack."

"I'd advise you to back off, Sidney," warned Cleary, his gut beginning to tighten as he caught sight of the wild glitter in Joe's eyes.

In addition to being as angry as a gorilla on a bad day, Sidney also demonstrated he was too dumb to recognize good advice when he heard it. He roughly reached into Joe's outer pocket and discovered that Roller Derby players were blessed with fast reflexes. Joe spun around and grabbed the huge legbreaker who demonstrated further stupidity by going for his gun. Joe beat him to his own shoulder holster, pulled out Sidney's .38, and leveled it at him.

There was absolute silence in the room, like the calm before the storm, broken only by the panting breaths of Joe and Sidney. Cleary heard his own voice break the silence like a distant roll of thunder. "Take it easy, Joe," he said softly. Joe's eyes focused on him with only faint recognition, but that was better than nothing. "That's right, just calm down. Let's all have a drink and talk about this."

Joe held the gun as though it were a foreign object, rubbing the barrel across his forehead, his stance like an animal at bay. "What the hell's going on here, Jack?" he asked in a distant, confused voice. He stood in the middle of The Crescendo Club, but Cleary knew Quinlan wasn't completely aware of either time or place.

"We'll sort it out, Joe. Just be careful of that gun. It might have a hair trigger."

But Joe was struggling to sort it out for himself. "Nothing's been the same around here since the war. Since these bloodsuckers moved in here with their guns and five-hundred-dollar suits. We shouldn't even be in the same room with lowlifes like these, Jack. You know that, don't you?"

"You're talking yourself into a jackpot," warned Mickey, his Peter Lorre eyes looking meaner than ever.

"Shut up!" yelled Joe, swinging the gun toward Mickey, his voice and eyes murderous.

"Put it down, Joe," said Cleary. "It's not worth it. You've got a choice. This time you got a choice."

Joe switched his attention back to Cleary. "I sure do, don't I?" He thought a minute, and Cleary dared to hope that maybe, just maybe, the whole situation could be resolved without anybody bleeding.

Joe turned to Mickey. "You know, I was going to pay this fat bastard back because you went to bat for me"—he hesitated—"now, I'm not paying nothing."

Cleary thought for a moment the problem would become academic, because judging from the swollen veins in Mickey Gold's neck, the mobster was in the midst of an apoplectic fit. A second later he decided it was a good thing he didn't go into medicine, because he would have made a lousy doctor. Mickey didn't expire in the middle of his melting cherries jubilee, but half rose from his chair and pushed the table over.

Joe raised the gun, and Cleary grabbed his shoulder. "Don't do it, Joe."

Joe bared his teeth in a man-eating grin, snapped open the revolver and extracted the shells, letting them drop noisily to the floor. Tossing the gun aside, he spread his legs and raised those large hands. "Come on, Mickey," he crooned. "Come on and try me."

Mickey, Cleary noted, was smarter than Sidney. Recognizing that Joe would like nothing better than to beat his brains and other more delicate portions of his body into mush, Mickey sat down. "I'll pass," he said, his eyes promising death and dismemberment at the earliest opportunity.

"I thought so," said Joe, turning back toward Cleary. "I'm sorry I got you into this, Jack. But remember, I didn't ask for any help."

Cleary watched him leave, a battered survivor of wars, public and private. No quarter asked and none given. Just like a certain private detective named Jack Cleary, he thought bitterly.

"We'll be seeing ya, Quinlan," Mickey yelled after him. The pudgy mobster moved to the bar, delicately blotting his face with a napkin. "Sidney, I want you guys to take care of this first thing in the morning."

Sidney looked like a boy who'd just opened a birthday present and found exactly what he wanted inside. "Right, boss."

Folding the napkin in half and brushing at a speck of cherries jubilee on his jacket, Mickey turned to Cleary. "You know, we used to have a lot of these wild-haired young guys running around the Strip,

Cleary. There ain't none of them around no more. They're all dust. Same as your friend's going to be."

Cleary ripped the napkin out of Mickey's hand, rage blurring his vision until only Mickey's face was in focus. "You know I'm not going to let that happen, Gold. How would you like the Vice Squad to raid your gambling dens every night? Pick up your numbers runners? Hassle your pimps? How would you like the Health Department and Fire Department to issue citations to your nightclubs for public health and fire regulation violations? Roaches in the kitchens, bad wiring backstage? Wouldn't sound good in the newspapers, would it? I can still do it, you plump little slug. People downtown still owe me a few favors, and they don't like you. I don't like you. You're a bloated toad, living off the nickels and dimes from the poor suckers who don't have the sense to know something's rotten when they smell it."

"Hey, I'm a businessman. I provide a service—" began Mickey.

"I know. You're just General Motors," finished Cleary, almost wishing he had that loaded revolver in his hand. Almost.

"I don't get it, Cleary. The guy's not your cousin or anything," said Mickey plaintively.

"I told you, he's a friend."

"All right, let me think a minute. I gotta weigh my options."

"I'm generous. I'll give you two minutes," replied Cleary, feeling a pall of darkness settle in at the edges of his mind. He had lied to Gold. Joe wasn't just a friend; he was the flip side of Jack Cleary. They were both suckers looking for black-and-white choices when life had faded to gray.

Mickey came out of his mental computations and snapped his fingers. "Give us a minute," he said to the mice and lizards serving him. He waited until everyone had moved off, then turned to Cleary. "You ever hear of a guy name of Frank Tucci?"

Cleary turned the words over, looking for the trap. "The New York crime boss," he answered cautiously.

Mickey nodded. "He's taking over a spot on the Strip. I need someone like you to act as kinda a go-between with him and me. I'll pay you, say three times your normal rate. *And* your friend Quinlan's off the hook."

Cleary saw the trap and sidestepped it. Black versus white. Clear-cut choice. No gray areas. "Go-between? For Mickey Gold and Frank Tucci? You forget who you're talking to, Gold?"

Mickey waved the question away. "This Tucci's an animal. Nobody can talk to him. He'll listen to you."

"If he's an animal, what does that make you, Gold? You're both just rats fighting over the same garbage can. Get yourself another errand boy." He ground out his cigarette with deliberate care. "And stay away from Joe Quinlan."

He was nearly to the door when Gold's voice stopped him. "What's wrong, Cleary? Can't even compromise your sacred ethics for one lousy week?"

Cleary turned. "Gold, you wouldn't know an ethic if it bit you in the ass."

Mickey's eyes were as cold and hard looking as the asphalt pavement in front of the club. "You can jack me around if you want. Send your friends from Public Health. Let 'em find cockroaches as big as horses. Pick up my hookers. I'll have them bailed out and back on the street in an hour. You can deal me some misery, sure, but your buddy won't be around to laugh. I did you a favor by forgetting the vig, and giving your boy another chance. He blew it. Now you owe me a favor. Think about it, Cleary. Quinlan's dead meat otherwise."

T H R E E

Cleary leaned back and noticed something different about his squeaking leather chair. It seemed to fit him. And it wasn't only the chair that was different, he thought, forcing himself to view his dead brother's office objectively. His books on local Los Angeles history were lined up beside Nick's tomes on electronics, useful if one did a lot of wiretapping, psychology, and the California criminal code. The latter was useful in keeping detectives out of jail for tapping phones.

Other than the books, he noticed other changes. Nick's desk was no longer neat. Files were stacked on one side. Napkins and matchbooks, covered with his own scrawl, were tucked under the blotter. Many of his clients associated a spiral notebook with cops.

Consequently he had learned to jot down notes on whatever was handy.

His coat was tossed over a chair back, spare packages of cigarettes were scattered on top of filing cabinets, bookcases, and the windowsill. A large wall calendar with cryptic notes hung in place of a painting. The office wasn't exactly untidy; it was just more lived in. It looked like him, not his brother. Nick had been an everything-in-its-place, round-cornered sort of guy. Jack Cleary's corners, on the other hand, were more knocked off than rounded.

When did it happen? he wondered, looking around at the changes. When did Nick's possessions suddenly become his own? Not when Nick was murdered, and not for several weeks afterward. It was still Nick's chair, Nick's desk, Nick's office, Nick's detective agency. Until when? Last week? Yesterday? Or last night when he looked in the mirror over the bar at The Crescendo Club, and accepted what he was? Provisionally. Provided he kept his right to choose between black and white. That right was in danger of being compromised, which explained why Charlie Fontana was sitting in a private eye's office after hours, and drinking said private eye's booze.

"I know you guys go back a ways, and I'll put him under protective custody if you want. But he'd lose my guys going around the block," said Charlie Fontana, sitting in sweaty shirtsleeves and pouring himself another drink from Cleary's office bottle.

Cleary got up and stepped to the window. Turning his head, he studied his old partner from the LAPD. Charlie Fontana didn't look like a cop if you ignored the gun tucked in his shoulder holster. His slightly square face was honest and open, a little sad looking maybe, but still an all-American boy grown up to be an accountant, or law clerk, or pharmacist, or cashier at the local bank. Anything but a cop. Until you looked at his eyes. Fontana had a cop's eyes. Cynical from dealing with rats like Mickey Gold, weary of the citizens' stupidity, despairing of the violence and filth that infested the Strip like fleas on a mangy dog. But honest. Charlie Fontana had honest eyes that even held a little hope if you looked deeply enough.

Cleary wondered what his own eyes expressed. Sure, he believed if you just kept slugging it out with the bad guys and made the right choices, eventually everything would work out. Maybe. If you kept your fingers crossed and didn't catch any lead in a vital area. If that was hope, then he had some.

He tapped his fingers on the desk. Hope was missing from Joe Quinlan's eyes. Joe kept fighting, but he didn't have any hope. And a man without hope doesn't care if he gets killed or not. It was Cleary's job to keep Joe Quinlan alive until he did care again. And Charlie Fontana wasn't being very helpful.

"Jack, have I got a wart on my nose? You're staring at me like I do," said Fontana, looking worried. That was another thing about Fontana, Cleary thought. He worried a lot.

"I was just thinking."

"Did you hear what I said about Quinlan? He's too slick to tail."

Cleary took a drag on his cigarette. "Yeah. You got any better ideas, Charlie?"

Fontana opened his mouth to answer, or maybe it gaped open in amusement. Cleary wasn't sure. He would bank on amusement, though, because the sight of Dottie's generous behind decked out in a skintight dress and squashed against the plate-glass front office door was worth a big smile of appreciation.

From the second pair of arms visible through the plate glass, Cleary judged Dottie was caught in the throes of a monster kiss. He was surprised she found the strength and coordination to reach behind her back and open the door. She even walked, or stumbled, into the office and managed to straighten her clothes at the same time. Cleary had underestimated Dottie's physical dexterity.

"Ooh, I love French movies," said Dottie to her escort.

Cleary recognized his secretary's date from the recent publicity shot she had begun displaying on her desk. He was one Vinnie Alberts, two-bit actor, wearing pleated pegs, matching two-tone jacket and bucks, and weighed down by an experimental thirty-weight pompadour. Hell, everybody under thirty was trying to imitate that new singer from Tennessee. What was his name? Elvis something?

"Don't you just love them, too, Vinnie?" continued Dottie. "They're so"—she hesitated—"*como se dice*." She searched for just the right word, and as usual scored a near miss. "Continental."

Vinnie nodded in agreement, snapping his gum at a hundred and fifty rpms as he moved in to cop a quick feel. Vinnie was strong on actions, but a little short on words, Cleary noticed.

Dottie slipped awkwardly out of his clutches and reverted back to Cleveland, Ohio. "Whatta you been on the range too long?" she asked in a nasal tone of voice as she realigned her uplift bra, which was on a down drift.

Vinnie snapped his gum and sneered. Or at least Cleary assumed Vinnie sneered. It was hard to tell when the greaseball's lip seemed to have a permanent curl to one corner.

Dottie caught her faux pas, and immediately shifted into her Leslie Caron personality. "We have all evening, Vinnie. Que sera, sera..." She looked up and choked.

Cleary glanced at his watch, then cocked an eyebrow at her. "Your apartment closed for remodeling, Dottie?"

Dottie pulled Vinnie's coat back on his shoulders. "I, uh, forgot"—she nearly dislocated her neck looking around—"my Kitty Kallen record."

Grabbing the record off her desk, she pulled Vinnie by his sleeve back out the door. His face hadn't changed expression, so Cleary was sure the lip curl was permanent. Probably a birth injury when Vinnie's mother tried to tie him in a tow sack and drop him in the river.

Dottie stuck her head back in. "Anything else I can do?"

"Good night, Dottie," said Cleary.

She gave an embarrassed shrug and softly closed the door.

Fontana looked at Cleary. "What'd you say that girl's name was?"

"Dottie."

Fontana took a sip of his drink, his face serious. "Her mother must've been clairvoyant."

"I'm not, but I know Joe's in way over his head, Charlie, and he doesn't care. They might just kill him," said Cleary, forgetting Dottie and her boyfriend.

"Not if you take Mickey's offer."

"I don't believe what I'm hearing. You must have had a couple of belts before you came off duty, not to mention the inroads you've made in my winter supply of bourbon. You forget we used to put guys like Mickey Gold and Frank Tucci away."

Fontana looked directly at him, and Cleary noticed his eyes were different. More cynical. And desperate, as if hope were in danger of dying. "We used to try, Jack. Tucci's one smooth bastard. Nobody's come close to nailing him. Every time we get a grip on him, he wiggles away like a greased pig."

He took a step closer to Cleary, his voice as earnest as his face. "Mickey Gold's dropped an opportunity right in our laps, one you'd have given your right arm for when you were in the department. It's a chance to bring down Frank Tucci before he gets a foothold out here, and set Mickey Gold back a good five years. It may be the only chance we get, Jack."

Cleary moved restlessly, then met Fontana's eyes. "I don't collect my paycheck from the city anymore, Charlie."

Fontana's eyes held a cautious expression that Cleary didn't like. "I know that."

"So forget about it."

Fontana nodded, then smiled. "Fine. It's forgotten. You're a civilian. Can't expect civilians to be crime fighters."

Cleary turned to gaze out the window at the lights of the restless city below. Then turned back to see Fontana's smile. That smile irked the hell out of him. It was hopeful, as if Cleary were some kind of super-hero coming to save the town.

"And even if I was going to consider something like that"—he watched the hope in Fontana's eyes grow—"it'd just be to get Joe out of a bad jam. I'm not Superman, Charlie. I don't look good in tights. And I wouldn't want any of those grunts of yours from

Metro on my tail. Guys like this can smell a backup a mile away."

Fontana misplaced his smile. "Whoa, wait a minute, Jack. You're the one talking like Superman. You think you can just walk in there like you can't be hurt? Gold and Tucci are smart, and both are like nitro. A slight shift in room temperature can set them off, and you'll be sitting square in the middle. Go-between for two killers, no backup, and no room for errors."

Cleary felt bitterness draw the skin taut over his cheekbones. "And I'm the match, Charlie. You can't have it both ways. Either I set them off, and you pick up the pieces, or Gold and Tucci will divide up this town like a pie. I'm the only choice you got, so we'll play it my way." He turned back to the window. "If I decide to deal myself in."

Fontana's answer was a long time coming. "You'll deal yourself in, Jack, because you can't stand by. And not just because of Joe Quinlan. Oh, maybe you owe him something I don't know about, but that isn't the debt that's eating your guts out. It's that Chinatown mess five years ago—"

"Shut up about Chinatown!" said Cleary, hearing the raw pain in his own voice.

"You didn't make a difference then, couldn't maybe. The choices were there to make, but you got dealt a bad hand. You were too young, and too soft to go for the tough decision. You hung on to believing in happy endings a lot longer than most of us. And if you'd made the other decision, it probably wouldn't have changed what happened. But you're always looking for a way to make up for it, Jack. I don't know if Quinlan's going to balance the score, but I do know you'll try to save his ass just because you didn't save that girl."

Cleary gripped the windowsill and stared blindly out. Fontana was right. He couldn't walk away this time. "I'll think about paying Gold a visit tomorrow morning."

"Jack, I don't want any of the pieces I pick up to be yours. Play it cool."

"You know, Charlie, five years ago you could see where the lights ended at the edge of town."

In Mickey Gold's Black and Tan Club, a bartender stacks chairs in the background as Mickey sits at his table, sipping a large glass of milk while he counts out the night's receipts with Meyer Alliance. Sidney Bloom, his bruises turning purple and yellow like decaying flesh, drops a small metal strongbox on the table. Mickey quickly stuffs the money into the box, his pudgy fingers not lingering on the bills. He is not interested in the bits of green paper themselves, but only in the power over others they represent. He has been without money before, and can survive without it, but he never intends to be without power again. Power means respect, and he likes respect. Jack Cleary's got no respect, and neither does that asshole Quinlan.

Sidney snaps the strongbox closed. Mickey makes a final notation on the cocktail napkin and slides it over to Meyer. No need for a copy. He will remember the figures. He has a good memory, always has had. And a long one. Mickey Gold never forgets anything. Or anyone. And he never lets anyone off the hook, just baits it better. Camouflage, like in the army. Question is, will Cleary recognize the camouflage, or will he take the bait? If he takes it, Mickey Gold will have a double fillet: Jack Cleary and Frank Tucci. Then he will pick his teeth with Joe Quinlan's bones.

He looks up to find Meyer and Sidney waiting respectfully. He nods and tosses Sidney the car keys. He watches them as they leave the room, turning off some of the lights as they go. They're good boys: loyal, dependable, respectful, boys. Up to a point. Mickey Gold never trusts anybody, man or woman, past the power he has over them.

Mickey takes a meditative drink of his milk and then goes back to making notations on the napkins. Maybe he ought to give Meyer and Sidney a bonus. Not a big one, no sense spoiling them, but a small one, tiny even, a token of appreciation. Businesses do it all the time. Gives employees some incentive to be even more loyal, dependable, and respectful. It's an interesting idea. He will give it some thought.

He hears a sound where no sound should be coming from and looks up. He freezes in middrink as Ralphie Santangelo steps out of the shadows. Mickey recognizes him as one of Frank Tucci's hoods, and is angered by the youngster's tanned good looks. Not much of a worker if he has time to lie around the beach. On the other hand, the way Santangelo raises the specially taped .38 says the boy is good at something.

After that observation Mickey puts visual impressions on hold and ducks as Santangelo calmly fires four times, shattering the table Mickey is hiding behind, and transferring everything on top of it to the top of Mickey Gold's brand-new, eggshell-white suit. The mobster adds Ralphie Santangelo's name to the list of people who've got no respect.

Santangelo, a wisp of smoke curling out of the barrel of his .38, steps up to finish it when Meyer

Alliance and Sidney flick the lights on as they rush
back in. Santangelo hesitates a minute, then melts
back into the shadows. He holsters his gun reluctantly. He is tidy in his work habits. He likes to finish
what he starts.

Sidney and Meyer, each mentally making plans to
take over the kingdom and wondering what the other
is thinking, rush over to the still smoking table. Like
a fat, angry phoenix, Mickey Gold rises from the
ashes and broken dishes, ghost white, but miracu-
lously unharmed. The king is not dead, and Sidney
and Meyer shelve their plans.

Mickey Gold decides that Sidney and Meyer will
definitely get a bonus. Loyalty and respect deserve it.
He might even throw in an engraved gold watch,
plated, of course, just to show his appreciation. He
sighs. The cost of doing business was going up all the
time. Maybe he will skip the engraving.

FOUR

A young Mexican boy hosed down the sidewalk in front of the Black and Tan Club. The sun, peering through the smog like a tawdry whore in a cheap lace veil, caught the water droplets in its feeble light, making them glitter like cloudy diamonds. He meticulously moved the hose from side to side, sluicing into the gutter the cigarette butts, wadded-up napkins, used-up Kleenex, and the other hundred and one pieces of trash dropped by drunk, careless, sloppy patrons of the Black and Tan for someone else to clean up. All the while he stared at Cleary out of the corner of one dark brown eye.

Cleary grinned to himself. He well knew one tired private eye wasn't fascinating enough to hold the interest of one medium-sized boy. It was his car. Even on the jaded Strip, a gleaming black on black '57 Cadillac Eldorado convertible with a chrome explosion of grille, Sabre wheels, and predatory tail fins, still caught the eye. Add the dual quad high-compression, full-bore 365, and racing suspension, and it was one hell of a car.

He slid out and gently closed the door, ran his hand over the soft leather upholstery, and winked at the boy. "You can touch it, kid, but careful with the fingerprints. It's the only thing I own I'm proud of."

The boy dropped the hose like it had suddenly turned into a snake, wiped his hands on his faded jeans, and carefully touched the hood ornament with one brown forefinger. "I'll be careful, mister."

Cleary grinned again and walked into the Black and Tan, wondering if he had ever been that young. Not in a long time, he thought, stretching his lips into a thin-lipped line as he caught sight of Mickey Gold.

"Cleary, come in, come in. Sidney here was just making a liquid repast, a pick-me-up, you might say. Would you care to join me?"

"I just drink with friends, Gold," Cleary said, eyeing the mobster, resplendent in starched shirt, tie, gleaming diamond cuff links, tiepin, and pinkie ring that altogether cost more than the Eldorado. "Besides, I want to keep my waistline where I can see my toes without bending over."

Gold managed a belly laugh about as false as his smile. "You're a real comic, Cleary. Ever thought of doing a nightclub act?"

Cleary caught the sudden flash of an expression in Mickey's eyes, but like the flick of a lizard's tail, it disappeared too quickly to identify. "No. I like to play to an audience of one."

A loud grinding sound like an engine without oil came from the blender Sidney was manhandling with all the grace and style of a baboon. Mickey pushed him aside. "You're gonna ruin it, you bum. You know how much these things cost?" He dropped in a few unrecognizable ingredients and turned it on. "Take a chair, Cleary," he said over the sound of the blender.

Cleary pulled out a chair and sat down to watch Mickey's usual three-ring circus. Sidney, a hurt look on his bruised face, hunched his way over to a table where Meyer Alliance was working on a half-dozen tout sheets. Sidney moved like a man with taped ribs. Wingtip damage, thought Cleary without any regret. He should've known better than to go for his gun and try to get up at the same time. Muscle-bound leg-breakers weren't known for agility.

He glanced around the room and wondered what happened to Mickey's special table. There was an empty space where it usually sat. The little slug probably made the mistake of leaning on it, he thought.

"Why don't you talk to Tucci yourself, Gold?" he asked.

Mickey watched the blender with unusual attention, punching the buttons on the small appliance like a kid playing with a toy typewriter. "Nah, I go over there and I'll just get acid indigestion."

Cleary smiled with his first feeling of enjoyment since he had walked in. "He's really got you worried, doesn't he, Gold? Don't want to think about him because you're afraid of losing your appetite?"

Mickey yanked the lid off the blender before it stopped grinding and jumped back from its splattering contents. "Goddamn it!" He examined his clothes for damages. "My dry cleaning bill's going to be three figures this month." He looked up at Cleary. "Well, I got a right to be worried. When he moved into Vegas, everyone thought it was for the low humidity. But in less than sixteen months, one Francis Michael Tucci had taken over three hotels on the Strip."

"They're still finding Moe Fein's body parts along Highway 91...." Sidney's voice trailed off as Mickey shot him a look. Cleary was surprised the bodyguard didn't drop dead right on the spot.

Mickey took a sip of his concoction, and turned to Cleary with another false smile. Cleary had seen used-car dealers selling stolen cars as previously owned who looked more honest. "You got a rep as a straight shooter, and Tucci's a businessman. He'll listen to reason. All you got to do is ask him what he wants to settle this."

Cleary straightened, his face tight. "Let's get our terms settled first. I talk to Tucci and you forget about Joe Quinlan? Is that the deal?"

Mickey took another swallow of the pink glob. "Yeah, yeah. Absolutely."

Cleary rose from his chair. "You got yourself a deal, Mickey." He walked half the distance to the door before he turned around. "You welch, and I'll come after you. And your ribless wonder with the space between his ears won't be able to stop me."

"You talking about me?" asked Sidney, certain he had been insulted, but not sure how.

Mickey touched his chest, his eyes wide and innocent. "You stab me to the heart, Cleary."

"You don't have one, Gold. And if you did, I still wouldn't stab you. I don't like you well enough to get that close."

He walked to the door, then glanced back. "By the way, you got a mustache around your mouth. Better wipe it off. Makes you look like a slob." He had the satisfaction of seeing Gold's face swell up and turn cherry red before he closed the door behind him.

He walked into the sunshine and watched the Mexican boy gazing mournfully at the Eldorado's dashboard. "Get in, kid, and I'll run you around the block."

The boy looked up. "But I got to do the sidewalk."

"It'll still be there when you get back," said Cleary, opening the passenger door and waving the boy into the car.

Mickey grabs a napkin and wipes his mouth as he watches Cleary leave. "Son of a bitch's got no respect." He turns to Sidney and Meyer. "No respect," he repeats.

"He's a real bum," says Sidney in one of his more brilliant observations.

"Shut up, Sidney," says Mickey, sliding into a booth and picking up a clean napkin. He begins making notations in his crabbed, awkward hand. He taps his pencil against his expensively capped teeth. "This Joe Quinlan might end up solving a big problem for us."

Sidney's face looks like a kid who's been told he can't go to the ball game. "Too bad. I was looking forward to seeing how he skates with two broken legs."

Mickey doodles on his napkin, drawing stick figures with the heads cut off. "Skates? Guy's a little big for the Ice Capades, ain't he?"

Sidney does a double take. "Capades, nothing. I'm talking Roller Derby."

Mickey's cheeks quiver as he laughs. "Roller Derby! That ain't no sport for a grown man. Does he chew bubble gum and collect baseball cards, too?"

"Hey, don't laugh, boss. It's a hell of a popular

sport. They're expecting a gate of more than twenty thousand for the Silver City Indians match tomorrow night. I got tickets. And Joe Quinlan's their star. He's dynamite on skates. He makes the wheels smoke."

Mickey shakes his head. "This guy's mental or what?"

Meyer clears his throat and pushes his glasses up. "It's a twenty-five-thousand-dollar, winner-take-all grudge match, Mickey. Lots of dough is going to change hands." Meyer only looks like a statistician. He talks like a thug.

Mickey's eyes light up like neon dollar signs. He rubs the side of his nose and considers. There may be a way to gain some respect from Joe Quinlan after all. "Where can we find this punch-drunk Roller Derby star?"

Cleary lit a cigarette and looked up and down the street. The smog wasn't bad this far out in the San Fernando Valley. The sun was hot and bright, the grass green, and the kids fat and healthy on this tree-shaded street of suburban tract homes, post–World War II models built on G.I. loans and the American Dream. He tried to imagine Joe Quinlan in this setting and failed. It would be like trying to hitch up a plow to a thoroughbred.

"It was his idea—suburbia. He thought a couple of orange trees and a white picket fence were going to make everything right again," said Eileen Quinlan as if she were reading his thoughts.

Her voice quivered and she turned to watch two matrons pushing strollers stop to examine a lawn mower. "It works," she called to them. "You're welcome to start it."

The matrons wandered off to look at a table loaded

with knickknacks, and Eileen saw Cleary checking out the amount of furniture and household goods stacked on the lawn. "Just having a yard sale to get rid of a few things that have been cluttering up the house."

Cleary didn't believe her. "Things like beds and all your living room furniture?"

She bit her lip and looked away, picking up a black-and-white photo of Joe and herself. Cleary recognized it; he had taken it just before Joe and he had been shipped out. Joe in his World War II uniform and Eileen in a bright yellow dress holding her hat with one hand while Joe bent her over his arm in a kiss like Valentino in *The Sheik*. They both looked so damn young and hopeful.

"I never met anyone like him, Jack. He was so full of life," she said, taking the photo out of its silver frame and laying it aside on a table. "I guess that's what kept me married to him for twelve years." She stuck a price tag on the picture frame and set it on another table.

Eileen was talking as if she were a widow, Cleary thought as he studied her face. She must be in her early thirties, still pretty, still athletic, but at the same time, she seemed old, plain, weathered; sucked dry by the emotional roller coaster called Joe Quinlan.

Eileen touched the photo with a shaking hand. "He was never the same after the war, Jack. And when he re-upped for Korea, I knew I'd lost him."

"The war changed us all," he said, reaching for the right words and knowing he hadn't found them.

"I know that. Most of you grew up, but not Joe. And it's not like he's trying to be like he was before the war. It's more like he's frozen into what he was during the war." She looked at him, her eyes puzzled. "Am I making any sense?"

"More than you know," he said, his stomach beginning to churn. He knew exactly what she meant, and he knew exactly who was responsible. And his name was Jack Cleary.

He looked around at the bargain hunters going through the yard sale items, selecting and discarding according to some pattern known only to themselves. Taking another drag on his cigarette, he surveyed the table that held the photo. It was a shrine, cluttered with the remains of her life with a man she couldn't understand.

"You're leaving him, aren't you?"

Eileen nodded and looked away, but not before Cleary saw a sheen of tears in her eyes. "It's over, Jack. God knows I've tried, but"—she drew a shaky breath—"I love him too much to watch him touch bottom. I'm going to Nebraska. I've got a sister there, some other family. I'll have another chance."

"That explains it"—he caught her questioning expression—"the look in his eyes these days."

She scraped her teeth over her bottom lip and clenched her hands together as if gathering her strength. "He still thinks we can make it." She drew another breath. "We can't. Not unless he changes. I used to try to fit into whatever plans he had, but he changed them too fast. I'd depend on one dream, get used to it, and he'd come up with another. And there were other women, Jack, like he was trying them out, too. All of it together was too much. We ended up with no dreams to build on."

She looked up at him, her wide brown eyes those of a wounded survivor. "He doesn't live here anymore. He's got a room behind the skating rink."

Cleary ground out his cigarette. "I already looked there."

A patina of new lines seemed to form around Eileen's eyes. "He's in trouble again, isn't he?"

He put his arm around her and kissed her forehead to avoid answering. What was the point? She had had a corner on worrying about Joe Quinlan long enough. Time for someone else to take over. "Do you have any idea where I can find him?"

"It's his birthday tomorrow, Jack."

Cleary nodded. He knew exactly where Joe was. And he didn't like it.

"It was his birthday when it happened."

"I know it. I was there. Hell of a thing to happen on your eighteenth birthday. But how did you know? You didn't meet him until afterward."

She looked across the lawn at nothing. Or rather at something he couldn't see—like a hopeful young girl in a bright yellow dress, and a young man in a uniform. "Birthdays were always bad for him, Jack. He always went on a binge. Once I even went so far as to hide all the calendars in hope the day would be past before he realized it. It didn't work. It was like he had some kind of alarm clock in his head that went off on one particular day. The first birthday after we were married, he disappeared for three days and I didn't know where he was. I nearly went crazy worrying about him. He came back home hung over and sick and apologetic. It was the war and I knew he was due to be shipped out, so I didn't do anything like walk out. But I did demand to know what had happened. He told me part of it, and his mother told me the rest before she died. I'm sorry it happened to him. It was horrible and tragic. I've tried to be understanding and forgiving, but what good does that do when he won't forgive himself?"

She pushed a strand of thick auburn hair off her face. "He's been going out there a lot lately," said Eileen, twisting her wedding ring around and around on her finger, but never quite taking it off. "Sometimes he's better when he comes back, but most of the time he's worse."

"I Walk the Line" reverberated across the rooftops as a bald, dirty white baseball smacked against a wall again and again in a frantic tattoo of sound. Cleary stepped out onto the tar-paper roof and stood quietly, listening to the grunts of exhaustion and the sound of footfalls, and watching Joe Quinlan play a game of baseball against the wall. The rooftop was smaller than he remembered it being as a kid. Part of the building jutted upward another floor, so it really was more like half a rooftop. And some of that was taken up with the little building that housed the elevator cables, one wall of which Joe was using as a backstop.

A portable radio, cranked up all the way, sat on the roof ledge, but Cleary doubted that Joe even heard it. It was just background noise to drown out the sounds echoing in his head. The *dreams* of sounds, rather. Because Joe had never really heard his sister scream. When they found her, huddled against that same wall, she had been dead more than an hour. Cleary remembered how the blood, sticky to the touch, had looked black in the moonlight. He remembered something else, too. He remembered that was the first time he saw the wild, angry look in Joe's eyes.

Stripped to the waist, body dripping sweat and smeared with dirt from impact with the rooftop, the

Roller Derby star played his solitary match as if his life depended on it. Or his sanity. The police never caught the murderer-rapist, and neither had Joe Quinlan. He had been looking for a target for all that anger ever since. Killing a baseball was better than killing someone else. Or himself.

Joe made a lunge for the ball and somersaulted across the tar paper. "Who's winning?" asked Cleary.

Joe looked up and smiled. "The home team."

Cleary reached down and yanked Joe back on his feet. "You weren't being very smart last night, pissing off Mickey Gold like that."

He was wasting his breath, Cleary decided, because his comment had about as much effect as spitting in the ocean. Joe bounced the ball up and down in his hand, then suddenly threw it across the rooftops, watching it until it disappeared in the distance.

Cleary tried again. "I'm going to have my man, Johnny Betts, stick with you a couple of days." If the stupid bastard wouldn't protect himself, someone had to do it for him.

Joe picked up his shirt and wiped the sweat off his face. "You're not worried about last night are you? Come on, Jack. We've fought tougher guys than Mickey Gold and his stooges."

Cleary lit a cigarette. "War's over, Joe."

"To hell with the war. What are you doing, Jack? I never asked for your help."

"You never could." Cleary heard the echoes of gunfire, the harsh tonal sounds of the enemies' language inside his own head, and forced them back into his memory. "You're my friend. There's some responsibility here."

"Responsible Jack Cleary, making everybody's

choices for them. Who the hell ever appointed you as my keeper?"

"Well, damn it, you're making a mistake. You made a mistake ever getting mixed up with Mickey Gold, and you're making a bigger one thinking you can thumb your nose at him and not get it knocked off."

"You think so?" Joe asked as he walked to the roof's edge and stared across the fifteen-foot chasm to the opposite building. He leaned over the ledge and looked out over the city, then down at the dizzying twelve-story drop to the pavement below.

He glanced back, and Cleary stiffened when he saw the wild look in Joe's eyes. "You know, I can still make it, Jack. Just like when we were kids. Do you remember when we were kids?"

Cleary wet his lips, and tried to sound calm. "Come on, Joe, of course I remember, but we're not kids anymore."

With a distant smile in his eyes, Joe started to back away.

"What's it going to prove, Joe...?" demanded Cleary, letting his voice trail off in midsentence, his features tightening as Joe started running toward the chasm.

"Joseph!"

Cleary grabbed for his friend and closed his hand around empty air as Joe took a half-dozen powerful strides and launched himself off the ledge. "Jesus Christ!" he screamed as he watched Joe, suspended in midair twelve stories above the ground, straining for all he was worth.

Cleary heard himself panting for breath as Joe barely made it. Grasping a hold on the opposite ledge, Joe lost his grip for an instant, then pulled himself up and straddled the ledge. "I told you I could still do it."

"What the hell does it prove, Quinlan?" Cleary yelled.

Joe faced Cleary over the man-made chasm. "It proves I'm still alive. That they haven't dragged me down yet, Jack." He tilted his head back, and a wild Tarzan yell echoed across the rooftops. "Not me. Not yet."

FIVE

**Saturday Night
L.A. Thunderbolts vs. Silver City Indians
25k Winner-Take-All Extravaganza**

Cleary glanced at the Olympic Auditorium scoreboard, then back at the lone skater whipping around and around the empty oval. Like the baseball game on the rooftop, like the leap across the chasm, skating against an invisible jam was another way Joe Quinlan competed against himself. What wars he fought, he fought alone. He would neither ask for help, nor accept it if it were offered. Which meant, thought Cleary, that any deal to get Joe off the hook would have to be made without his knowledge. And that left

Jack Cleary with no options. He would meet with Frank Tucci because he had no other choice.

Reaching into his pocket, he removed a wire recording device and handed it to Johnny Betts. "Here, hold on to this wire for me. I better go clean to the first meet." He looked at his watch and stood up. "I better leave. I don't want to be late to my first appointment with crime's answer to Superman."

Johnny's brown eyes held a worried expression Cleary knew Betts would deny. "Watch yourself, huh. From what I hear, this Tucci is a for-real nut who gets his jollys rubbing people out. I can't go around breaking in new bosses every week. Takes too long to show you the ropes."

"I can take care of myself, Betts."

"Yeah? Well, I heard different. I heard you're always sticking your neck out, and someone's always got an axe waiting."

"I wear an iron collar, kid." He nodded his head toward the skater. "Just stay with him and make sure he doesn't get in the middle of this."

He turned to go when Johnny's voice stopped him. "I gotta ask what your angle is here, Cleary. What do you owe this guy?"

Cleary looked at him, then through him, to a time Johnny Betts was almost too young to remember. "It goes back a ways . . . to the war."

Johnny snapped his fingers. "Don't tell me: he took a bullet for you, saved your life. Now you're eternally grateful. Right?"

"Wrong." Cleary's lips were numb from the ice-cold tone of his own voice.

Cleary docked his Eldorado in front of Frank Tucci's futuristic, Lautner-designed house perched high above the city. Just like an eagle's aerie, he thought as he slid out of the car. Except he didn't like comparing Tucci to something as noble as the eagle. He wondered if vultures built nests in high places. Because one thing was for sure. If Frank Tucci was in L.A., it wasn't for the scenery.

Ralphie Santangelo walked up and rested his hand on the Eldorado's hood. "You're on time."

"Time's money," said Cleary, checking out Ralphie's clothes to see what the well-dressed thug was wearing in the tag end of the 1950s. "Hands off the car, please. Fingerprints ruin the wax job."

Nico Cerro, an Old World button man, cold, efficient, and also well dressed, materialized at Ralphie's side. "Touchy, aren't you?" he asked, running his hand down the Eldorado's side.

Cleary suspected these two and he weren't going to be best friends. "Just particular about who touches the merchandise."

Nico didn't like that because his cold, dead-looking eyes turned a little colder and looked a little deader. "Come on. Mr. Tucci's waiting."

Cleary waved his hand. "Lead on, Macduff."

Nico and Ralphie gave him a blank stare.

"Not students of the classics, I guess," said Cleary.

"Shut up, Cleary," said Ralphie, leading the way up to the floor-to-ceiling glass entrance.

"Nice house," observed Cleary.

With a jerk of his head, Nico motioned Cleary to follow. "Mr. Tucci's at the pool."

"Nice day for it," said Cleary, wondering how well Tucci could swim with a pair of handcuffs around his ankles, then remembering he didn't have any with him. He would have never lived to tell about it, anyway, he thought, as Ralphie and Cerro ushered him up a staircase, onto a covered sun porch, past an art deco—style outdoor bar, to a table occupied by the vulture himself.

Cleary decided he was maligning the name of vulture as he took stock of Frank Tucci in slacks and sport shirt sipping from a tall glass of ice water. Frank Tucci was a snake, a hooded cobra maybe, who ruled by stealth and fear, striking out with deadly fangs at the first sign of unexpected motion. Watchful, unblinking black eyes studied him until Cleary felt a stab of sympathy for a cobra's prey. The bastard's eyes were damn near hypnotic.

Tucci signaled toward a chair with a flick of his wrist. "You may sit."

Cleary shook his head. "I'll stand. I like to keep my options open." He also didn't like snakes and didn't want to sit close to one.

The wavering aquamarine reflection from the pool danced across Tucci's face, blurring his expression. "I did some checking on you. Silver Star. Decorated ex-cop who can't be bought. Word around town is Jack Cleary's a right guy."

Tucci spoke in a low, modulated tone, as if weighing every word, and with only a hint of a New York accent. Ice rattled in his glass like dry bones each time he drank. "Check him," he said to Nico, his serpent's eyes fixed on Cleary.

Cleary hardly heard the words before Nico struck, patting him down with impersonal efficiency, leaving a cold spot everywhere he touched. Cleary considered kicking him in the balls, but postponed it until a more auspicious time when he didn't risk getting his head blown off.

"He's clean," announced Nico in a flat voice and

stepped back to stand watch like a minor serpent, not as deadly as Tucci, but no garter snake, either.

"I have to ask you something, Cleary. Why are you working for Mickey Gold and his matzo ball Mafia?" asked Tucci, his snake-cold eyes unblinking.

Cleary shrugged and straightened his jacket. "It's a quick couple of grand." He caught sight of the cold disbelief in Tucci's eyes. "Gold doesn't want another war on the Strip, and neither do I. Makes it difficult to have a quiet drink after work. The sound of guns and firebombs disturbs the peace and tranquillity of my favorite bar."

Tucci smiled, a stretching of thin lips until his fangs showed. "War? I don't know what you're talking about. I'm opening a nightclub."

"Just like you opened nightclubs in Havana and Las Vegas? I heard there's more in the cornerstones than cement."

Tucci feigned surprise. Almost successfully. "Mickey's not worried about a little friendly competition, is he? Such lack of patriotism. This country was built on the free enterprise system."

"I don't think the Founding Fathers had using .38s and firebombs as business tools in mind."

Tucci took another drink to the accompaniment of the dry-bone rattle of ice cubes. "You exaggerate."

"Gold wants to know what you want."

Another thin-lipped smile. "What do I want?" Tucci asked, as if he couldn't believe Gold was so stupid as not to know. "I want what everyone wants. More. Tell Mickey Gold I want more."

Johnny sat in the stands in Olympic Auditorium, watching Joe Quinlan work out on the oval by himself. Or maybe not by himself, thought Johnny. Quin-

lan, dressed in tattered old sweats and shorts Betts
wouldn't use to wax his '49 Merc, and wearing a
thick, clumsily taped knee brace, worked out against
some ghost no one else could see. He sped around
and around the oval, dipping low on the turns, using
the full momentum of the banks to build speed, then
hurdled himself against an invisible jam. The sound
of Joe's skates, and his accompanying eerie war cry
like a sad and angry Indian, echoed loudly in the
huge empty hall, and gave Johnny the shakes. Joe
Quinlan might be Cleary's friend, but he was weird,
man.

Joe screeched to a sudden stop and tested his bad
knee. Picking up a roll of tape, Joe began retaping it,
soundless whistle pursing his lips.

"What happened to your knee?" Johnny asked.

Joe winced as he pulled the tape taut around the
knee. "You name it, kid."

Johnny scratched his ear. Quinlan was as close-
mouthed as Cleary. "You and Cleary go back a ways,
huh?"

Joe tore the tape off and adjusted the brace before
looking up to study Johnny. Betts had the feeling Joe
might just as quickly knock his ass off the bench as
talk to him. He let out a breath as the older man decided which. "You were the kid out here last night
with Jack Cleary."

Johnny couldn't decide if Quinlan was asking him
or telling him. Either way, he might as well introduce
himself. "I'm Johnny Betts. I'm supposed to hang
around, sorta check out your back the next couple
days."

"And if I tell you to take a hike?" asked Joe.

"Hey, man, I take my orders from Cleary. He tells

me to lay off, I will. Otherwise, you got a new shadow."

Quinlan grinned. "Cleary was just about your age, maybe a little younger, when we first started knocking around together," said Joe, biting off the end of the tape, and tossing the roll back on the floor.

Johnny adjusted his collar until it stood up in back. High style. "Hard to imagine. He's kinda cast in stone, you know. Like he never was anything but right. What was he like then?"

Joe looked out over the empty auditorium. "Wild. Stubborn. Real independent." He turned and smiled at Johnny. "Kind of like you, kid." He straightened and skated lazily into the tunnel. "Think on that while I grab us a couple of cold ones."

Mickey Gold shifts uncomfortably on the metal folding chair. He scoots it further back into the shadows and looks with distaste on Joe Quinlan's makeshift living quarters. A cot, a broken mirror, an old locker with its door off substituting as a closet, and pictures of some woman on the wall. He compares it in his mind to his own immaculate home, and feels rage interfere with his indigestion. Joe Quinlan, living in a room a skid row bum wouldn't be caught drunk in, and he still has no respect for Mickey Gold. Impossible. Intolerable. That's what comes of letting someone off the hook. If you lose control, you lose respect. Mickey Gold doesn't like to lose either one.

He watches Joe skate inside and glide to the Coke machine. Joe lifts a tire iron off the top of the machine, inserts it in the dispenser, gives it a crank and, at the same time, smashes the machine with a bottle-rattling slap. A bottle magically drops from the machine. Mickey Gold nods with approval. He likes ingenuity. Besides, he never pays a machine himself. It's against human nature.

Mickey Gold tenses as Sidney Bloom materializes out of the shadows and Joe wheels on him with the tire iron.

"You wanna piece of me? Here I am," says Joe, a wild look in his eye that Mickey doesn't like.

"Take it easy, Quinlan. We're here to make life a lot easier for you. How'd you like to wipe the slate clean with us and put ten grand in your pocket on top of it?"

"What're ya talking about?" asks Joe, brandishing the tire iron.

Mickey relaxes. If Joe Quinlan asks questions, then he is halfway on the hook. "I understand you got a big money match tomorrow night." He sees something surface from deep in Quinlan's eyes, and promises himself an extra cherries jubilee as a celebration treat.

S I X

Cleary heard Johnny Betts before he topped the hill and saw him leaning against the fender of that eyesore Merc, killing time by polishing his side mirror and adjusting the aerial for better reception on his car radio. In Cleary's opinion, better reception didn't improve the rock and roll music endangering Bett's hearing and the neighborhood's peace. Jesus, how could he listen to that crap hour after hour without getting a headache?

Johnny looked up as Cleary's Eldorado glided to a stop. "Hey, man, everything's cool. Not a hood in sight."

Cleary looked at Eileen Quinlan's house for a moment, then back at Johnny. "Sidney Bloom could blast

Joe, dig up the patio with a jackhammer, bury him with a twenty-one-gun salute, and you wouldn't hear a damn thing over that radio."

"Me?" he asked, pointing to his chest with a thumb. "I got ears like a cat, man."

"Yeah, a deaf one. Go drape yourself around the doorknob."

"Maybe I ain't gonna win a good citizenship award, Cleary, but I'm no Peeping Tom."

Cleary pitched his cigarette into the street and took a deep breath. Sometimes Betts tried the patience of a saint, and Jack Cleary never claimed to be a saint. "I didn't tell you to look through the keyhole. I just want you to stick real close to Joe tonight. The second meet's set with Tucci. A couple of hours and this will all be over. I don't trust Mickey Gold to keep his word if Joe Quinlan's running around like a lamb ready for the slaughter."

Johnny rocked back on his heels and laughed. "Lamb! If that guy's a lamb, I'm Little Bo Peep."

"Betts!"

Johnny spread his hands, palm upward, in a gesture of innocence. "All right, all right. No sweat. I'll be on him like white on rice. Or wool on a lamb."

Cleary nodded and started his Caddy. "Just keep him under cover and quiet as you can."

Johnny wondered if they were talking about the same guy: Wild Man Quinlan, who thought a fistfight was a social engagement. "Hey, Cleary," Johnny said.

Cleary sighed and shifted into neutral. "Yeah, Betts?"

"Fontana backing your play?"

Cleary patted his jacket pocket. "I'm going to get everything on this wire. I don't want to take any chances of Tucci spotting one of Fontana's units."

Johnny put his hands on his hips. "That's just great, man. That's so damn stupid, I can't believe it. What if Tucci searches you? You think he's not going to recognize a wire? Hell, he'll fill you so full of holes, we can strain tea through your hide."

Cleary impatiently tapped his fingers on the steering wheel. "I'll leave you the detective agency, kid. At least, it'll be one way to make you get a haircut and wear something besides that leather jacket."

"Quit cracking jokes, Cleary!"

"Just relax, kid. I've been around the track a few times. I know what I'm doing."

Johnny nodded and fidgeted like the kid Cleary accused him of being. He opened his mouth several times, until Cleary wondered if he had suddenly lost his voice. "Look, Cleary, uh, about last night. I was way out of line." He fiddled with his aerial for a minute, then turned back, white lines of anger bracketing his mouth. "I've been backing your play since day one here, and I just thought you might want to cut me a slice and let me know what exactly is going on. I mean, you're sticking your neck out a mile. What the hell do you owe this guy?"

Cleary sat with eyes fixed on Johnny.

"Oh, shit, just forget it," said Johnny, turning back to his aerial. But not before Cleary saw the hurt expression in the younger man's eyes.

"Joe didn't save my life. I saved his."

Hearing a familiar chime, he looked up to see a Good Humor truck surrounded by excited children parked down the street. He remembered one hot, sticky night on some hellish Pacific island that was infested with bugs big enough to carry you off. The humidity was so high you could wring water out of the air, and the Japs had the whole company penned down in the lousiest stretch of jungle on the whole island. He and Joe had spent the hours talking about the first thing they were going to do if they ever got home in one piece. Joe had wanted a cone from the Good Humor man.

Cleary switched off the Caddy's motor and got out. He pulled a coin out of his pocket and tossed it in the air. "Come on, kid. I'll buy you an ice cream."

Johnny trailed after him, silent for once, which was just as well, thought Cleary, paying for the cones and retracing his steps back down the bucolic street. He needed a few minutes to think just how to explain to a confused kid who'd never been to a war. He glanced around at the sprinklers lazily spraying the lush suburban lawns and thought how different it was on that island.

"Joe and I had been eating dirt behind a fallen palm tree for most of the night, shooting at anything that moved. And there was a lot that moved. Those islands were crawling with a lot of things besides the Japs. I never saw so many lizards in my life. They dropped out of trees onto the back of your neck. They crawled out of the underbrush. You could damn near find them in your canteen. I still get the creeps when I see a lizard."

Involuntarily he shivered. He would never forget listening to the rustling of leaves, and the tight feeling in the gut while you wondered if what rustled had four feet or two. "Anyway, we were penned down, but the Japs couldn't dislodge us. Finally, about daylight, we were overrun by two battalions of Nippon Rangers. Crack veterans with a suicide complex. They didn't care if they got killed as long as they could take a few of us with them. You couldn't just wound them. You had to kill the bastards. By the time we got our orders to fall back, there was a stack of bodies in front of that palm tree and Joe was already hit—his knee."

Cleary took a deep breath, thought for a minute he could smell cordite in the air, then continued. "I don't know if he wanted to die on that island. Maybe he had some idea what he was coming back to." He wiped his mouth, tasted the sandy grit of that island again. "He wouldn't fall back, just kept firing, that wild look in his eyes like he was a suicide squad of his own. I had to knock him cold to get him out of there."

Johnny licked his cone, his eyes mirroring his confusion. "But it sounds like he owes you. Not the other way around."

Cleary shook his head. "You got to understand. Joe Quinlan was always a hero. In high school. Football." He watched the Good Humor truck drive slowly up the block. "He was made for the Glory Days. He should've gone out a hero like everyone expected. Instead"—he heard the bitterness in his voice—"instead he came back to this." He waved his arm at all the perfect suburban lawns. "Things had changed. There was nothing to struggle for, nothing to measure himself against except how much thicker his grass was than his neighbor's, or how much bigger his bank account was."

Johnny stood looking at Cleary, his cone melting in the hot sun, running over his fingers, and dripping onto the ground. "Just because you save someone's life, you can't be responsible for what he does with it. You can't keep chasing after him wiping up his messes."

Cleary let his shoulders slump. "Don't you see, kid? I took away his choices on that island. He didn't choose to come back alive. I chose for him. Now, I'm responsible." He clapped Johnny's back. "Just stick with him, huh? And get up closer to the house. Mickey Gold's whole mob could hide in that shrubbery."

Shaking his head in disbelief, Johnny watched Cleary drive off in his black Eldorado. Jesus, that guy was nuts. The men in white coats ought to take him in and teach him how to weave baskets. Anybody with any brains at all knew that if you did a favor for somebody, he owed you. But trust Cleary to get it all screwed up. He needed a keeper, somebody to see he stayed out of trouble and away from bad company like Joe Quinlan. To get caught between two mobs just to save a war buddy was a sure sign of softening of the brain. All the same, he thought as he trudged up the sidewalk to Eileen Quinlan's house, he would rather have Cleary in his corner than the heavyweight champion of the world.

He skipped the porch. No hood, even one as dumb as Sidney Bloom, was going to walk up to the front door for all the neighbors to see, ring the doorbell, and blast whoever answered. If anybody was going to ventilate Joe Quinlan, he would come up the alley and through the backyard. He worked his way down the front of the house, checking the bushes for hoods and noticing the roses had aphids. He had worked for a landscape artist for a couple of months until he got caught doing a little heavy petting with the guy's daughter, and if there was one thing he recognized, it was aphids.

There was one other thing he recognized, he thought as he caught sight of Joe Quinlan and Eileen through the open living room window, and that was a man who felt as if he were a stranger in his own house. He had had some experience along those lines, too. Every time his dad want to jail.

He felt sorry for Quinlan, standing there in the doorway, holding his gym bag and watching his wife fold clothes as if it were the most interesting thing he had ever seen. Poor guy didn't look as if he wanted to admit that she was jumping off his bandwagon. And judging from the mess the wife was making out of folding those towels, she wasn't looking forward to making him admit it, either.

Johnny started to slip past the window. He had done all the eavesdropping he intended to do. He wasn't a pervert that stood around listening to other people's troubles. Feeling a tug on his sleeve, he looked down to remember one other fact about rose-bushes: they had thorns. And ninety-five percent of all the thorns on this particular rosebush were buried in his black, genuine leather, steel-studded jacket that cost him most of what he earned spraying aphids for two months.

As he disengaged the rose's teeth from his jacket, he heard Quinlan speak. "I know I lost a lot of myself along the way, but I always had you."

He stopped, and Johnny saw him look toward the ceiling as if the right words to say might be printed there. "You're the only thing I have. Don't leave me, Eileen. We can work it out!"

Eileen turned around, and Johnny saw she had been crying, probably for a long time. Her eyes had that red swollen look that spelled more than one cry-ing jag. "I love you, Joe. I do, but I can't stay and watch you lose a little bit more of yourself every day. You're on an island in the Pacific, or up on that roof-top beating yourself over the head because you never found whoever killed your sister so you could beat them instead. You can't be a hero every day. Sometimes you have to compromise and be an ordinary man."

She wiped her eyes, and Johnny was afraid she would start crying again. He saw Quinlan take a step toward her, but she waved him away. "I've got a ticket out of here first thing tomorrow morning."

Quinlan looked stunned, as if he had been punched in the gut. Or as if he saw the ground drop out from under his feet, thought Johnny. "Just give me another six months to scrape up the cash," he heard Joe say. "We'll get that place we always talked about. Forty acres overlooking Seneca Lake."

"*Don't!*" said Eileen violently. "Please don't. I know you really mean it. At least for now, but I've heard the same make-believe dreams for twelve years. I'm not a make-believe person. I need some real dreams even if they're not the kind we used to share."

There was more, but Johnny couldn't stand to listen. Ripping his sleeve loose, he ran back to the Merc, piled in, and slammed his fist on the horn until he saw Joe leave the house, looking alone and desperate. He grabbed a copy of *Roller Derby* magazine and buried his nose in an article until Joe climbed slowly into the car.

"You gotta cinch up tight tonight, man. These Silver Indians are on the warpath. According to this, they put three Golden Bombers in the hospital last week," said Johnny, careful not to talk too fast. He always sounded guilty when he talked too fast, and he didn't want Joe thinking he knew anything. Which he did. More than he wanted to.

Tossing the magazine into the backseat, he switched on the motor, glancing sideways at Joe. He pushed in the clutch, shifted into first, and drove off, wondering if the other man was going to explode all over his front seat. Looking at Joe again, he changed his mind. Cleary's buddy wasn't going to explode. He was going to—what was the word—implode, collapse into himself, like an inner tube with a puncture. If he did, Johnny figured there wouldn't be much left of Joe Quinlan. The guy was empty already. Better get Joe's mind off his woman troubles and on to his game, or the Indians would wipe the track with him.

"What's up, champ? Don't tell me you got a case of the pregame jitters? Listen, you just watch your skating, and you'll be fine," said Johnny, tapping his fingers on the steering wheel and trying out a grin.

"I need to make a phone call," said Joe, his voice and face totally expressionless. Like a wooden Indian, thought Johnny.

"Sure, champ," he replied, swerving into the curb and stopping in front of a phone booth.

Johnny slid out of the Merc, opened a bottle of Coke on his belt buckle, and sat on his fender, his back to the phone booth. He lifted the Coke in a toast to a couple of greasers working on a custom '55 Chevy and shifted his body so he had an unrestricted view of the phone booth in his side mirror. Tapping his finger in time to "Rock Around the Clock," he watched Joe insert a coin and dial a number off a matchbook cover. He squinted, but couldn't see the name on the matchbook. Man, talk about a Peeping Tom, he thought. He couldn't even let the guy make a phone call without spying on him. But damn it, who would he be calling? Joe Quinlan didn't have any friends except Cleary.

He took another sip of Coke and watched Joe pound the phone with his cast when it returned his coin. Champ sure wasn't calling out for Chinese. A guy doesn't rearrange a phone booth because he can't reach his favorite carry-out restaurant. Johnny watched Joe redial, then turn around. Man, he wished he could read lips, because Joe was banging his cast on the phone again and didn't look very happy with the conversation. He finished his Coke as Joe slammed the receiver down. It bounced off the hook and jerked at the end of its cord like a jumping jack. That guy was weird. He wished Cleary had steered clear of him, because Joe Quinlan was trouble with a capital T.

The Black and Tan Club is empty. Clean white cloths cover the tables, napkins are folded, silverware laid out, glasses sparkling on the bar, carpet freshly vacuumed. It is a stage, props all in place for the hipsters looking for action, the starlets looking for contacts, the lonely businessmen on the make.

The houselights dim, an actor's voice echoes from the shadows. "How much cash can we lay our hands on in the next two hours?"

A spotlight flashes on and illuminates Mickey Gold, his hand resting on the phone. Gold turns his head, and another spotlight picks up Meyer Alliance, sitting alone with his adding machine, punching numbers and making notations in a ledger.

"We've got just over eighty-six thousand in the safe," says Meyer, his voice as dry as the paper money that is his life. "And we can scrape up another eighteen thousand and change if we pick up the West Side number's take."

Like a malodorous Buddha holding court in sordid splendor, Mickey Gold smiles at Meyer. It is a self-satisfied smile, a cruel smile, the smile of a man who achieves an unworthy goal. "Put it all on the Indians for tonight, Meyer. I told you everybody has their price." He pats the phone. "Quinlan's throwing the match."

Mickey clams up at the sound of approaching footsteps. The stagelights come up and he pastes on a look of jolly evil as the main character makes his entrance, escorted by Sidney Bloom.

Cleary stepped into the empty nightclub, glad he could feel the hard, reassuring weight of his .38 in his shoulder holster. When dealing with rats like Mickey Gold, it was a good idea for the exterminator to carry something besides traps. Particularly when the chief rat had an enormous grin on his face. That always meant bad news for someone.

"Did you cheat a widow out of her husband's insurance policy, Mickey?" he asked. "Or is that grin for me?"

The grin turned into a sneer that Cleary considered more becoming. "Well, well. If it isn't the Dag Hammarskjöld of the underworld."

Meyer and Sidney gave the joke a bigger laugh than Cleary thought it deserved. But if you worked for Mickey Gold, it was safer to laugh at his jokes. He shot them a look he used to reserve for axe murderers and child abusers, the look that said one more word, and I'll cut you up with a dull saw. The look still worked, he noted with satisfaction as the two thugs choked off their laughter between one giggle and the next.

Cleary turned back to Mickey. "Don't push your luck, Gold. I'm the only thing standing between you and Frank Tucci. Make me angry, and I'll let Tucci spread you the length of Mulholland Drive." He eyed the mobster's plump form. "And he wouldn't even have to spread you very thin. You're packing enough fat to grease both lanes for five miles."

Mickey misplaced his grin. "Did you forget our deal? Tucci for Quinlan?"

"I haven't forgotten, but I don't like what I'm doing. Give me the least excuse, and I'll take a powder. I'll figure out another way to get Joe off your hook. Like chop your fishing pole into pieces."

Mickey wiped the sweat oozing out of his pores. "Okay, okay. You set the meet? Right?"

Cleary nodded, wondering what Mickey had up his sleeve besides his lumpy arm. He had given in too quickly. He should've wiggled and squealed like a trapped rat, gnashing his teeth and biting everyone in sight. "Yeah. I'm going up to Tucci's place tonight."

"You sure he'll be there?" asked Mickey anxiously.

Cleary frowned as he studied the mobster. "He'll be there. He wants to hear your terms."

Mickey pulled a napkin out of his pocket and checked it. "Just tell him if he lays off my numbers in the south bay and leaves me half the vending and pinball machines in Hollywood, I'm going to give him all of my East and Central L.A. territory."

"Without a fight? Since when did you become Santa Claus, Gold? What are you keeping back?"

Mickey got up, his chair creaking in appreciation of being relieved of Gold's weight. He slung his arm around Cleary's shoulders, smothering him in after-shave and the smell of evil. "You're a smart guy. I mighta known you wouldn't buy my charity act, so I'll let you in on a little secret, Cleary. We got knocked off at two of our wire services last month. We had a couple of our runners hit by one of these kid gangs springing up all over the place since the war. It's not like the old days. People are losing respect for the old order. We got anarchy in this country. Goddamn Communists are undermining society."

"My heart bleeds, Mickey."

"Let Tucci get the ulcers. It'll leave me more time to soak up the sun at my Palm Springs place."

Cleary shrugged off the mobster's arm, making a mental note to decontaminate himself at the earliest opportunity. "I hope you got a high fence around your pool, Mickey. The sight of you in a swimsuit will ruin the tourist trade down there," said Cleary, but his heart wasn't in it. His head was throbbing like a bongo drum. Worse than it usually did around Gold.

Mickey held up one hand. "Scout's honor, Cleary. I'm playing you straight."

Cleary pressed his fingers against one temple. "You couldn't play straight if you had a ruler, Gold, so I'll ask you again. After tonight's meeting, Quinlan is off the hook?"

"Absolutely. After tonight, my problems with Tucci will be over."

Gold was caving in like a tin roof in a hailstorm. And Cleary couldn't remember the last time it had hailed in L.A.

SEVEN

Man, but these guys are big, Johnny Betts thought as he visually measured the broad back of one gladiator pulling on a size 48 jersey. He stood beside Joe at the door to the Thunderbolt locker room and watched the solemn athletes prepare themselves. Tape was wrapped around strong, scarred fists; pads were pulled onto elbows, knees, forearms, and banged into place. A player's thick forearm smashed a locker door shut, leaving a dent in the metal surface. Skates hit the floor, feet jammed inside and laced tight by thick, callused fingers. Helmets were pulled on, framing the thoughtful, distant faces of hard men about to do a violent act for a buck.

"Hey, man, is it the Christians against the lions, or

what?" asked Johnny, his voice breaking an absolute silence. "These guys are gearing themselves out like they expect to draw blood. They're doing everything but filing their teeth. Are they always this revved up?"

Joe jerked his head at a huge Sioux wearing war beads and an eagle feather in his hair and busily taping down his forearm pad with the concentration of a brave checking his supply of arrows for an upcoming massacre. "Hey, Nicky, what's going on?"

Nicky Whitehorse looked around at the other players as if he were taking a vote. Several nodded, and Nicky, elected spokesman, turned back to Joe. "We haven't done anything real in a long time. The guys pooled everything they got for this one. Tiny over there"—pointing to a looming giant with a size 20 neck—"put in the money he was saving for his honeymoon. We lose, and him and the bride's gonna bunk down in the backseat of his Chevy."

The Thunderbolts wordlessly skated out past Johnny and Joe. Nicky stopped in front of Joe and held out his fist, all taped up and ugly as a mutant mummy's. Joe knocked down Nicky's fist with his own in what Johnny presumed must be some kind of pregame ritual like slicing your chest or wearing war paint.

"We're gonna do it . . ." said Nicky in as close to a growl as Johnny figured the human voice was capable of making.

"Till the blood flows," agreed Joe, moving past Nicky toward his locker. He tore off his shirt, revealing a torso with more scars than a twenty-year-old neighborhood tomcat, and opened his locker.

Johnny saw him pick up an envelope and open it. "You getting fan mail, champ?"

Joe stuffed the envelope back into the locker under

his spare jersey. He glanced over his shoulder at Johnny. "Yeah, they leave me letters in the damnedest places. One dame hid an invite to her hotel room in my extra jockstrap." He laughed, but Johnny noticed it didn't reach his eyes.

Johnny punched Quinlan on the arm, but softly. No point in stirring up the animals. "I'm going to grab me a seat right down front, champ. Crunch a few for me. I'll see you in the winner's circle."

Joe pulled his number 43 jersey over his head, and gazed at the younger man until Johnny squirmed uncomfortably. "Sure, kid. Enjoy the game."

Johnny tried to figure out just what kind of look Quinlan had given him. Desperate, disappointed, scared, mad, thoughtful. He discarded the last guess. Joe Quinlan didn't look like the kind of a guy who thought much. He just reacted.

To hell with it, he thought as he squeezed into the seat next to Dottie. Maybe the guy was just upset because his wife was leaving him.

Dottie daintily took a bite of a chili dog, chewed, swallowed, and delicately touched the corners of her mouth with a paper napkin, her eyes swiveling from side to side. "I've got to thank Cleary for these tickets. I hear you can make a lot of contacts at one of these matches."

"What are ya talking about?" asked Johnny, looking around at the rowdy crowd. He didn't think there were any kind of contacts in this crowd that a nice girl would want to make. At least, not without checking out the results of their blood test.

"You know, show business types, producers and directors, people like that. They come to these matches and they're always on the lookout for a new talent. Maybe I'll get discovered."

"Oh, Lordy!" exclaimed Johnny as he spotted the Blond Bombshell, who was dressed with one thing in mind, and it wasn't Roller Derby.

"Well, it's not impossible," said Dottie, her full lips rounding into a pout. "Lana Turner got discovered in a drugstore."

The Roller Derby star shot Johnny a look he could chin himself on, and he smiled weakly and scooted closer to Dottie.

"I mean, you don't have to be so negative about it," continued Dottie. "This is L.A. Anything can happen."

It sure could, thought Johnny as he wrapped his arm around Dottie's shoulders, and hugged her. A man could get raped by a six-foot blond Amazon.

Dottie dropped her chili dog, barely catching it before it landed chili side down on her pedal pushers. "Are you touched, or what?"

"No, no," said Johnny, nuzzling her ear and peering at the blonde out of one eye. "You just look good to me tonight." At least he could get his arms around her chest with room to spare.

Dottie patted the mass of curls that served as bangs and preened, spotting the blonde leering at Johnny in the process. She self-consciously straightened up to look taller and pulled her shoulders back to compete with the Roller Queen's historic proportions.

"Quit wiggling," said Johnny. "I could keep a grip on a greased pig easier than you."

Dottie arched her back to push her own attributes to their furthest limits. "I'm not wiggling," she hissed. "I just don't want to slump, that's all."

Johnny glanced down at Dottie's uplifted bosom,

then at the Blond Bombshell who was doing a little
back-bowing of her own. "God help me," he muttered.

His prayer was answered as the crowd roared and
both women forgot their bosoms in the excitement of
watching Joe Quinlan thunder around the oval.
Nicky Whitehorse threw a bone-rattling block, free-
ing Joe who dipped past a swinging Silver City Indian. The announcer's voice rang out over the noise
of the crowd.

> And Quinlan gets by Baby Bob
> Bluewater. Look out, Waylon!

Quinlan dumped another Indian on the hard wood.
With quick, economic strides, he bore down on another waiting Silver City Indian defenseman. Johnny
covered his ears as the crowd competed with the announcer's voice.

> One more Silver Indian to go. Ten
> seconds to go in the second period.
> Can he do it? . . . seven . . .
> six . . . five . . . four . . .
> three . . . two . . . one . . .

Quinlan slammed back and forth into the huge defenseman, and Johnny was on his feet yelling. At the
last second Quinlan seemed to hesitate. The bell
went off and he was blasted against the rail. Johnny
joined the crowd in one long, collective groan. Even
the announcer sounded sympathetic.

> A-w-w, too bad, folks. Wild Man Joe
> Quinlan's bid falls a little short.
> Indians 24 . . . Thunderbolts 20 . . . at
> the end of the second period.

Johnny scooted to the edge of his seat. Quinlan was hanging on to the rail, his head down like he didn't have enough strength to raise it. Poor guy was probably trying to get his breath back from wherever that defenseman knocked it. He opened his mouth to yell something encouraging when the Roller Derby star looked up at someone in the crowd. Johnny turned his head in the same direction and froze. Mickey Gold was sitting in the row behind the scoreboard. And he was saluting Joe with his program.

"What the hell is going on?" said Johnny aloud.

"The Thunderbolts are losing," said Dottie helpfully.

"I know that! I mean, what's going on up there?" He saw Dottie's puzzled expression and waved his hand as if he were swatting a fly. "Forget it."

He half rose from his seat when he saw Nicky Whitehorse grab the rail next to Joe. "What the hell's wrong with you tonight, Quinlan? You should have blown right by that bum."

Damn good question, thought Johnny.

"You're skatin' like a damn sissy afraid he's going to fall down and go bang," continued Whitehorse.

"So I slipped up. I'm not goddamn perfect, you know," answered Joe.

Nicky punched Joe's shoulder. "You better be tonight. We need the Wild Man. Get the lead out and get in the game, man. This is our chance to win a little pride back," he said, and skated angrily off.

Johnny got up and took three steps to the rail. "You'll get them next period, champ." You better, or I'm gonna want to know what you got going with Mickey Gold, he added silently.

Joe's eyes narrowed. "You seem pretty sure about me, kid."

Johnny tucked his hands in his pockets. "Sure enough to put a C-note down on you." He saw that desperate look in Quinlan's eyes and turned up the heat. "Cleary told me when the chips are down, you can always put your last dollar on Joe Quinlan."

Like hell, he thought as he sat back down. Even if Cleary had said that, Johnny Betts had too much moxie to bet a nickel on somebody as close to doing some straightjacket time as Joe Quinlan. And to think that Cleary was rubbing noses with a killer just to help the crazy bastard.

He watched the pack set up in preparation for starting the period. Johnny shook his head in amazement. What a way to make a living. The Thunderbolts and the Indians looked as if they had already gone fifteen rounds with a meat grinder. He saw Nicky Whitehorse, winded and bleeding, nudge Quinlan, and he edged forward on his seat to listen.

"This is it, Joseph. Last chance to make up for all the lost years," said the big Sioux.

Last chance to play it straight, champ, thought Johnny as he looked over his shoulder at Mickey Gold. The mobster wore a grin like the cat that ate the canary, and Johnny knew his suspicions were right. Gold had something set up with Quinlan. Question was: would Joe Quinlan go through with the deal?

Turning back to the oval, Johnny saw Quinlan glance at the scoreboard, then at his teammates, then finally up at Mickey Gold. What's it going to be, champ? he wondered, and watched for a long moment until Joe Quinlan's lips spread into a wild, defiant grin.

"Let's cream these guys. Show 'em who's got guts," said Joe, and Johnny sank back in his seat and let out a breath he didn't know he had been holding. Then he started worrying. Joe Quinlan might have guts, but he wouldn't after Mickey Gold got hold of him.

The announcer's voice rang out in the auditorium.

> Hold on to your hats, ladies and gentlemen. This one's for *all* the marbles.

It sure is, thought Johnny. And Mickey Gold is going to be left holding the bag. The bell rang and he and the crowd sat back to watch as the teams jockeyed for position.

Joe sped around the oval in full heat of battle, took out one Silver City Indian with a tremendous blow, then tomahawked another one into the rail. Johnny ducked as the player's helmet flew by him and took out a spectator three rows back. The player himself crashed through the railing and did a midair somersault to land with a dull thud at Dottie's feet. She squealed and clutched her hands to her bosom. Johnny leaned over to check for signs of life, saw the Indian was still breathing but out for the count, and turned his attention back to the match.

Joe came off a turn, ducked under a swinging Indian and dumped him with a leg whip. The player did a hundred-and-eighty-degree turn on his back, slid under the railing, and knocked himself cold hitting the concrete floor of the auditorium.

The crowd began counting down the last seconds of the match as Joe came out of the last banked turn doing forty-five, and blasted past the last two Indians, dumping them both as he rocketed by. The two players landed spread-eagle on the wooden track. One climbed back to his feet on rubbery legs that promptly tangled together and dropped him across the chest of the other player, who lost all interest in returning to the game.

Johnny twisted around as the bell rang and the crowd went wild to check the scoreboard.

Thunderbolts 51—Silver City Indians 50

He saw Mickey Gold tearing up his program and glaring down at the oval track. Johnny discovered he could read lips after all, because he had no trouble figuring out what Gold was screaming even though he couldn't hear a word over the roar of the crowd.

"Quinlan, you're a dead man!"

EIGHT

Cleary ran his hand over the front of his jacket. Good tailoring counted when you packed a gun and a wire. A bulge where there shouldn't be one, and Snake Eyes Tucci would bite his ass. Or have Ralphie do it, which might be worse. Tucci and Ralphie were equally poisonous, but the latter was more likely to add a few annoying improvisations, like ripping off arms and legs.

He leaned one hand on the doorbell and the other on the sparkling plate-glass wall. Just a little annoying habit of his own, he thought with satisfaction as he smeared his palm over the glass in a series of swirls. He surveyed the results, added a few diagonal lines just to give the design some variety, and admired the results. Amazing what a little gun oil on the fingertips would do to glass. Juvenile, he knew, but it felt good, and there hadn't been much about this whole deal that felt good. Take your pleasure where you find it.

Ralphie Santangelo opened the door, and Cleary wondered who his tailor was. The hood's jacket hung crooked over the iron lump of his .38. Well, no one's perfect. "Good evening, Ralphie. Kicked any dogs or twisted any arms today?"

Ralphie locked the door with a viscious wrist motion that should have broken off the key. "You got a smart mouth, Cleary."

"That happens when a guy's bright."

"Watch out somebody don't shut it permanently," sneered Ralphie, his lips curling back from his teeth.

"Life is a risk," agreed Cleary. "Take me to your keeper."

Growls rumbled up from Ralphie's chest, and Cleary swore a strip of the thug's thirty-weight hair rose up like hackles on a mean dog. "It's gonna be a pleasure to put out your lights, Cleary, and I'm gonna do it one light at a time."

Cleary gave him ten points for eloquence. "Slip of the tongue, Ralphie. I meant take me to your leader."

Ralphie flashed him one last warning look, let his lip curl back over his teeth, and ushered him up the stairs to a room off the sun porch. It was designed as a living room for gracious living, but a futuristic desk shaped like a flattened kidney resting on two beer kegs dominated the space and spoiled the gracious effect. Flanked by Nico Cerro, Frank Tucci sat behind the desk, a businessman dressed in an impeccably tailored dark blue silk suit and crisp white shirt, accompanied by his trusted personal secretary. The

fact that Nico Cerro looked as much like a secretary
as Charles Atlas looked like a ninety-pound weakling
didn't seem to bother Tucci. Of course, when your
business is dealing in filth, not interoffice memos,
maybe Cerro was good casting.

Cleary stopped halfway to the desk, feeling all his
juvenile recklessness melt away like fog before the
sun. Tucci was too dangerous to bait. "You wanted to
know Gold's terms," he said.

Tucci made a graceful motion with his wrist, his
snake eyes black and glittering like the city lights visible behind him through the expanse of glass walls.
Cleary guessed vultures liked unrestricted vision, the
better to spot carrion. "Why don't you have a seat, and
we'll talk about Mickey Gold's future."

Cleary sat down carefully to avoid pulling his
jacket taut over his gun. "You're talking like the treaty
has already been signed, and you're ready to colonize
the conquered territory. There hasn't been a war yet,
Tucci."

Tucci smiled, a mere stretching of his lips that did
nothing to lighten Cleary's feeling of imminent doom.
"I am getting ahead of events, aren't I? An old habit
of mine, planning ahead. Let's hear Gold's terms first.
Then I'll decide if I'll accept his terms of surrender."
He took a sip of ice water, and Cleary decided he was
replacing the blood in his veins.

"Gold is offering you East and Central L.A. You lay
off his operations in the rest of the city. It's a good
split, Tucci. You both get half the pie, and nobody
spills blood."

Tucci stood up and turned to look down at the
sweeping vista of L.A., like a vulture looking over
road kill and trying to decide which part to consume
first. The gangster whirled around, his eyes looking

more alive than Cleary had seen them. "East and Central Los Angeles! He thinks that'll satisfy me?" His voice was harsh, the New York accent more noticeable. "I haven't heard word one about his laundry service, vending operation, refuse contracts. Mickey must think I'm a fool. And I don't like people thinking I'm a fool. It's not healthy. For them," he added, holding out his glass. "Ralphie, get me another ice water. Wasting my breath makes me thirsty."

Cleary lit a cigarette to give himself time to think. It wasn't that he really gave a damn whether Gold and Tucci ate each other up, but he still had too much cop in him to want a gang war to break out. And that was the real reason he was sitting in this plush room with an uncaged snake. He was as much interested in pinning a rap on two gangsters as in getting Joe Quinlan off the hook. He still had enough pull downtown to make things hot for Mickey Gold, and Gold knew it in spite of his blustering to the contrary. He was in this for himself, for Jack Cleary, because he wanted to make a difference, to make up for the time he didn't and a Chinese girl died.

"What are your terms, Tucci?" he asked, getting up and moving closer so the wire would pick up the gangster's voice. "I need something I can take back to Mickey Gold."

Ralphie handed Tucci his ice water, and the mobster sipped his transfusion. "My terms are simple and nonnegotiable. I want all the vending machines, including half of all of Mickey's action in Hollywood and West L.A., which will be under our control. Mickey will get his cut from us." He leaned over his desk. "I want to work out the details with Gold, personally."

Fontana ought to be pleased with that speech,

thought Cleary as he shook his head. "Gold says that this is going to be the last meeting."

"Last meeting? What the hell is that two-bit matzo ball trying to pull? Nobody tells Frank Tucci he won't deal, not if he wants his body to stay in one piece." Tucci broke off, his black eyes staring at Cleary like a rattler planning to swallow a rat. "What's going on here, Cleary? Why'd Gold send you up here if he wasn't planning to deal?" His eyes narrowed. "Unless he was setting me up." He snapped his fingers. "Ralphie, search him."

Ralphie started toward Cleary, a smile of pure enjoyment on his face, when a clicking noise distracted him. He turned toward the sun porch and the pool beyond. Cleary didn't bother. If there was one sound he recognized, it was the safety on a gun being flipped off. Being a cop taught you things like that. Sometimes it saved your life. Like now, he thought, as he ducked to investigate the plush carpet from a nose-length away just as two gentlemen in shiny suits and wraparound sunglasses cut loose with submachine guns, shattering the plate glass and decorating the opposite wall with a series of holes arranged in an abstract pattern.

"Goddamn it!" shouted Tucci from the other side of the desk where he also was enjoying a close-up view of his carpet. His reflexes weren't so good, thought Cleary, observing an oozing streak of blood on the side of the mobster's neck. Nice to know Tucci had blood instead of ice water in his veins.

"Cleary, you son of a bitch. I'm gonna spread your body parts from here to the Golden Gate!" screamed Tucci.

"I didn't have a damn thing to do with this," shouted Cleary over the sound of exploding glass and reverberating gunshots. He rolled over, saw long tongues of fire flash from gun barrels as the hit men spread another tattoo over the wall, and pulled his .38. He snapped off a quick shot, missed, and heard the deep bark of Ralphie's gun to his left. The first shooter flew backward into the pool where he added a red splash of color to the sparkling aquamarine water. The second hit man disappeared into the shadows.

Cleary climbed to his feet, his ears still ringing from the sounds of gunfire, just in time to see Cerro turn his weapon on him. Cleary hit the carpet at the same time he felt the heat of a passing bullet that shattered the only remaining pane of glass in the expanse of wall.

Cleary returned the shot, admired the adroit way Cerro ducked to avoid a new part in his hair, and climbed to his feet. "Call off your goons, Tucci. I'm not going to call fire on my own lines."

Tucci stared at him for the space of a heartbeat, but whatever he might have said was interrupted by Ralphie. "Hold it right there, Cleary," he said, his intentions as clear as if he had published them in the *Los Angeles Times*.

Cleary jumped through the shattered window instead. No point in hanging around where you weren't welcome. Shots made a lacy pattern on the leaves of the orange tree he was crouching under, and he silently slipped deeper into the shadows. Ducking from tree to tree, he rounded the house, pulled his car keys out of his pocket, and did a running dive into the Eldorado.

"Come on, baby," he whispered as he fumbled the key into the ignition. "I'll never ask another thing of you if you just show your tail fins to these bastards."

Baby must have heard him because with a deep

roar, the Cadillac started. Throwing the gear into reverse, Cleary backed downhill, shifted rapidly
through the gears, and headed toward Mickey Gold's.
He had a score to settle with the pudgy little rat, and
he planned to start by knocking the sleazy little matzo
ball's teeth so far down his throat, he would have to
take off his shoes to eat.

N I N E

Johnny Betts grabbed Dottie's hand. "Come on."

"Wait a minute! Where are we going? I was kinda planning on getting another chili dog and a Coke before the concession stand closed. Watching all those guys skate made me hungry." She hung back.

He tugged at her hand. "All that stuff will break your face out. Now, come on. I don't have time to argue."

"I did have kind of a little place when I woke up this morning. Right there." She touched her cheek. "Can you see it? About an inch from my nose?"

"Sure, and you'll break out like a kid with measles if you eat that junk. Now come on, or thumb a ride home," he said, dragging her along.

She tottered behind him on high heels. "But where?"

"The locker room. I gotta warn Quinlan."

"The locker room! But there'll be men in there undressing."

"Think of it as a new experience," he said, heading down the tunnel.

"Oh, doll face," called a husky feminine voice.

"God help me," he said under his breath. If it worked once, maybe it would work again.

Either God was busy, or didn't hear him over the racket of the crowd, because the next thing he knew, his arm was almost wrenched out of its socket. "Hey, sweetie," said the Blond Bombshell. "I've been looking for you. You didn't stick around after the match the other night."

Johnny swallowed. "I told you, I had to work."

"Your boss gave you the night off." The Amazon's big blue eyes narrowed into slits, and he noticed that her biceps were bigger than his. "I don't like guys standing me up."

"Hey, babe, would I do that to a hunk of woman like you?" he protested. "I was planning on us getting to know each other real well, but an emergency came up. I tried to get out of it, but my boss depends on me. I'm his main man, you know." He edged his way into the locker room.

"What do ya do?" asked the blonde.

"I'm a private eye, or rather Cleary is. That's the guy I work for. I do a lot of undercover work for him."

She ran a finger the size of a giant redwood down the middle of his chest. "Yeah? Well, undercover work's kind of what I'm interested in."

Johnny felt sweat bead on forehead and looked desperately at Dottie. "Then here's who you want to talk to. She's been with Cleary a long time. She can tell you all about it. Can't you, Dottie?"

But Dottie was staring openmouthed at a couple of semiclad Thunderbolts. "Will you look at that. I wouldn't have thought a Roller Derby guy would wear boxer shorts."

It wasn't much of an opening, but Johnny figured it was the only one he was going to get. "Hey, Dottie, Blondie here plays Roller Derby, too. Maybe she can introduce you around. Maybe you can get your picture taken with one of the guys for the newspaper. The press is looking for some good shots of the Thunderbolts."

Dottie latched on to the Amazon's arm like a leech and Johnny slipped his leash and escaped. "Can you introduce me to that one over there with the little red hearts on his shorts?"

The Blond Bombshell was looking at Cleary's secretary like she might at a caterpillar she caught crawling up her arm. Johnny refused to feel guilty. Dottie could take care of herself.

It was bedlam in the locker room as he pushed his way through the crowd to put as much distance between himself and the Roller Derby queen as possible. The players were celebrating their victory mostly by pouring cheap champagne over each other. The place sounded like the St. Valentine's Day Massacre with all the corks popping like gunshots. It was going to be Roller Derby Day Massacre if he didn't get to Joe Quinlan.

"Hey, champ," he called over the heads of a dozen sportswriters, but Joe, charged up like a battery and red from a combination of bruises and exertion, was too busy shaking hands and punching his teammates to answer.

Shoving his way through the crowd with elbows and his heavy motorcycle boots, he finally reached hailing distance of Quinlan, who was stripping off his uniform and pulling on street clothes like a quick-change artist. "Hey, champ"—he began.

"The Wild Man comes through," interrupted Nicky Whitehorse, holding a bottle of champagne in one hand, and punching Joe in the arm with the other. "Hey, what's the rush? We got some celebrating to do."

Joe tried on a grin that Johnny thought had a long way to go before it fit. "I think I might have made a couple of enemies out there tonight."

"Shit, man, all the Thunderbolts made some enemies tonight, but none of them's in any shape to do anything about it."

"These might be," said Joe.

Johnny finally made it to within reach of Quinlan and pounded him on the back. "Way to go, champ. Easiest hundred I ever made."

Joe threw on his shirt, stuffed an envelope in his belt, and looked at Johnny. "Did you really bet a hundred?"

Johnny looked at the floor for a second. He ought to say no, let him know that Johnny Betts figured out Wild Man Quinlan was about to throw the match. Make him feel lower than an ant's knees for even thinking about it. But he wouldn't. This was Cleary's buddy, and he would be way out of line to interfere. Besides, Quinlan had played it straight in the end, maybe even been kind of a hero because he had to know that Mickey Gold was going to take him apart for welching on the deal.

"Sure I did, champ," he began, when Nicky Whitehorse popped another cork on a champagne bottle. "Son of a bitch," he said instead as he jumped backward out of the spray. "Watch the jacket, man. It's real leather."

When he looked up, Joe Quinlan was gone. Glancing around the locker room, scrutinizing the faces of the raucous crowd, he spotted Mickey Gold and Sidney Bloom pushing their way to the back of the locker room. Climbing on top of a bench, he jumped over the back of a seated Thunderbolt and headed for Gold.

"Something wrong with the floor?" asked the player, grabbing his jacket and gazing at him with eyes pink from the effects of cheap champagne and sharp elbows.

"I'm looking for Joe Quinlan. He's a buddy of mine," said Johnny, pulling his jacket from the Thunderbolt's fist.

The hulking player blinked and grinned, exposing a gum line with several empty spaces. "Out the window. Just like Wild Man Quinlan. He's too crazy to use the door like everybody else."

Johnny looked toward the back wall, and found the open window. Mickey Gold had, too, and wasn't very happy about it. Gold pounded the wall until Johnny wondered if it would stand, or crumble into dust and bring the ceiling down on their heads. He couldn't hear what the mobster was saying, but his newly discovered lip-reading ability told him that none of it was anything a Sunday school teacher would like. Sidney Bloom made some comment, a stupid one if Johnny knew the bodyguard as well as he thought he did, and Mickey threw him a look that would've melted steel down to a gray puddle. The mobster turned and started elbowing his way through the mob to the back door.

Johnny turned around and tapped the drunken Thunderbolt on the shoulder. "Is there a back way out of here?"

The player tilted his head back and emptied half a bottle of champagne, belched, then jerked a thumb over his shoulder. "Over there," he said, turning his wobbly head. "That door the little dumpling and the big guy are opening. Goes out to the alley."

Johnny saw Mickey Gold and Sidney disappearing out the door. He wondered how Mickey would like being called a dumpling, then turned back to look at the crowd. People were thicker than fleas on a dog. He would never get out of the locker room in time to help Quinlan.

Urgently he turned back to the player. "I'll give you a C-note if you can clear me a path to the door." He grinned. He ended up losing that hundred on the Thunderbolts after all.

"All right," shouted the player, his skates hitting the floor followed by his weaving body. Putting his head down like a charging bull, he blasted through the crowd, slamming people to the left and right to the accompaniment of the sound of thick pads hitting soft flesh. Johnny followed in his wake, jumping over the crumpled, moaning bodies writhing on the champagne-wet floor.

Thrusting a hundred dollar bill at the drunken Thunderbolt who grabbed it, then promptly passed out, Johnny ran up the tunnel, out the auditorium side door and around the building to his parked Merc, taking a quick look up the alley as he passed. Joe Quinlan was standing alone facing two huge leg-breakers coming at him from one end, and Johnny didn't think it was to congratulate the Roller Derby star.

Jumping into the Merc and slamming the door, Johnny jammed the key into the ignition, turned it and pushed in the clutch. "Come on, baby, give me all you've got."

With an explosion of duel carbs kicking in, the Merc rounded the corner into the alley and the brilliant headlights picked up Mickey and Sidney standing behind Quinlan. "You must've taken one hit in the head too many to think you could get away with this," shouted Gold.

Joe Quinlan turned, and Sidney pulled his .38 and took careful aim.

"Get 'em, baby," said Johnny, and the Merc roared down the alley, French headlights and gleaming grille bearing down on the thugs like an avenging angel from Detroit.

Mickey and Sidney jumped backward into a stack of empty cardboard containers that collapsed on top on them. Johnny had just a second to observe that the containers were actually cartons, and originally had been filled with chili. Mickey Gold was sitting on his ass in a back alley splattered with globs of cold chili.

Johnny slammed on the brakes, and the Merc came to a shuddering stop beside Joe Quinlan. "Need a lift?" he asked, leaning over and flinging open the door.

Cleary slipped through the back door of the Black and Tan Club into the white plastered walls and polished hardwood floors of Mickey Gold's personal living quarters. His suit was dirty and rumpled, his face so long unshaven it was beginning to itch, and his eyes red and burning from lack of sleep. He felt like yesterday's garbage, and suspected he looked worse.

He was also angry. No, not angry; he was beyond that. He was enraged to the point that he saw objects through a red veil of fury. He understood now why someone would kill in a fit of passion. He was very close to that point himself. Very, very close.

He stepped backward into the shadows the barely risen sun hadn't exiled for the day and watched Sidney Bloom hurry down the stairs followed by Mickey Gold.

"Goddamn chili," said Mickey. "Even the cleaners can't get that shit out of a sharkskin suit. I'm gonna take the cost out of somebody's hide." He brushed at the lapel of another white suit with the brim of his Panama hat held in one hand, and lugged a heavy leather suitcase in the other.

Cleary smelled the hair oil and talcum powder emanating from the mobster, and felt his eyes start to water. "You smell like a pimp, Mickey," he said in a low voice, almost a growl.

Both hoods jerked their heads around, Sidney's chin connecting with Cleary's fist. "Clumsy," murmured Cleary as he nailed Sidney again, sending him sliding across the waxed floor to collide against a potted plant. At that point the bodyguard lost all interest in the proceedings as he settled down for a long stretch of checking his eyelids for cracks.

Mickey took a clumsy swing at Cleary with his heavy suitcase. "You're out of practice fighting, Mickey," said Cleary, catching the end of the suitcase and using it to smash the mobster back against the wall, knocking his Panama to the floor.

Mickey staggered over and picked up his hat. "This is a one hundred and sixty-five dollar Panama, Cleary."

"Too bad," said Cleary, slamming his open hand

across Gold's face, then hooking his arm around the mobster's plump neck.

Mickey grabbed the arm, but his street-fighting days were too far behind him. His muscle had turned to fat. "What's the problem here?" he croaked.

Cleary squeezed his arm tighter and watched the Peter Lorre eyes of the gangster bulge out a little more. "You mean aside from the fact that two of your shooters tried to rearrange my intestines last night?"

"I don't know what you're talking about." The sentence ended in a gagging sound as Cleary squeezed again.

"You used me, you son of a bitch."

"Hey, everybody uses everybody in this town. It's nothing personal."

Cleary jerked the gangster's head backward until Gold's eyes glazed over like a three-day-old dead fish, and his voice turned into a breathless gobble. "Honest to God, they were supposed to wait until you were out of the way. You know me, I never hurt anybody that didn't have it coming to 'em."

Underneath the smell of hair oil and cologne that rose like a noxious cloud from Mickey Gold, Cleary caught a whiff of fear. Compounded of acrid sweat and a certain sourness of breath, it fed the beast Cleary knew was as much a part of what he was as his determination to be a just man. He was tempted to unleash the beast, tempted to kill Mickey Gold, tempted to enjoy twisting the mobster's head until the vertebrae cracked. But he could not. Once a man took that first step and committed that first deliberate, cold-blooded murder, there was no turning back. The beast was free and could never be caged again.

He pushed Gold away, suddenly nauseous at even touching him. "You blew it, Mickey. You had your shot and you blew it. Tucci's going to come after you with everything he's got. And as far as I'm concerned, you got it coming."

Cleary walked toward the door, his shoulder throbbing from landing on Tucci's carpet, his legs aching from jumping out a window. He felt like an overage comic book hero racing around the city in a fancy car he couldn't afford, trying to make a difference. Hadn't Chinatown taught him the impossibility of that?

"Hey, Cleary. Don't be so damn smug," shouted Mickey Gold hoarsely. "You got a bull's-eye on your back now. Just like me."

Cleary looked back over his shoulder at the gangster. "Then I'll see you in hell, won't I, Gold?"

T E N

"Thanks for saving my ass, kid," said Joe Quinlan, belching up an onion smell. "And thanks for the smothered steak dinner." He patted his flat stomach. "Gotta feed the inner man after a hard match."

Johnny figured Joe Quinlan must have three men living inside his muscular frame because he put away enough food for that many. "Running from Mickey Gold kinda gave me an appetite, too."

"Yeah, well, it works that way sometimes," agreed Joe, and then fell silent as Johnny parked the Merc in front of Eileen Quinlan's house. It was barely dawn, but there was a light on in the living room.

"I'm going to ask you something again, kid, and I want you to tell me the truth," said Joe Quinlan as he and Johnny walked up the path to Eileen's house. "Did you really bet a hundred dollars?"

"Best hundred I ever spent," replied Johnny, wondering if the drunken Thunderbolt who'd cleared the path out of the locker room still had the C-note when he woke up.

Quinlan looked up at the sky and laughed. "I think you're lying kid. When you told me that cock-and-bull story, you were looking at me like I was lower than dog shit. You knew I'd made a deal with Mickey Gold. It took me a while to figure out why you didn't blow the whistle on me. It was because of Jack Cleary. You didn't care if the crowd tore me to pieces. You didn't care if Nicky Whitehorse scalped me right there in the infield. But you cared a whole hell of a lot about disappointing Jack Cleary. You'd have stood right there and let me throw that match if it meant Jack wouldn't find out his buddy was a cheat. You're a Boy Scout, you and Jack both."

Johnny shrugged. "I don't know what you're talking about."

"Sure, kid. You don't know a thing. Let me ask you a question." He pulled an envelope stuffed with bills out of his belt. "Supposing I had agreed to throw the match, and supposing Mickey Gold paid me half in advance. But then some kid said something that reminded me I used to stand for something, so I don't go through with the deal. Do you think I ought to give the money back to Gold?"

Johnny halted with his hand on the doorknob. "Hey, man, Gold probably cheated somebody out of that five grand to start with. Maybe he needs to know how it feels. Might make a new man out of him. Or give him a heart attack. Either way, he's better off."

"How'd you know it was five grand?" asked Joe suspiciously.

"I got a lot of skills: hot-wiring cars, opening locked doors, picking pockets. You're twenty bucks short, by the way. I figured if I saved your ass, you could pay for dinner."

Joe grinned and slapped the money against his palm. "Open the door, kid. I gotta save my life."

Johnny pushed open the door and stood back, feeling like an eavesdropper. But hell, he had been one before.

Joe walked into the empty living room as Eileen carefully set one last suitcase on the floor next to several others. "Do you believe in second chances, hon?" he asked, waving the money in the air. "What's wrong, Eileen? Why are you looking at me like that?"

Johnny could see the tiny white lines between her eyebrows as she looked from Joe to the door. "Where's Jack?"

Johnny felt the hair on the back of his neck stiffen at the urgency in her voice. "What's the problem?"

She looked at him, rubbing her hands together as if she were washing them. "A Lieutenant Fontana called looking for him. They haven't heard from him in a couple of hours. He sounded scared. I didn't know cops got scared."

"Damn it!' exclaimed Johnny. "That means trouble. I told him not to do it, but he wasn't about to listen to me."

Joe's eyes switched back and forth. "What are you talking about? He's probably out on the town with some babe. It's no big deal."

Johnny turned on him, all the disgust he had felt for Quinlan from the beginning flooding back. "Didn't you wonder where Cleary was tonight? Didn't you wonder why he didn't come see you beat the hell out of the Indians?"

"Wait a minute. He don't want to come, I'm not going to twist his arm."

Johnny stuck his clenched fists in his pockets to keep from decking Quinlan. "You don't even know, do you? Or don't you want to know? Cleary went to bat for you with Mickey Gold after you messed up."

"Yeah, I messed up, but it's none of Jack's business. I never asked him to stick his nose in it. It's my problem."

"Not to Cleary, it's not. He's your buddy, Quinlan, from the time you were kids, and you don't even know him well enough to know he's going to finish what he starts. He's stubborn, remember? You said that yourself. He made another deal to get you off the hook. While you were skating and playing games with Mickey Gold, Cleary was waltzing with a killer."

"Call Fontana back, Mrs. Quinlan. Tell him I'm headin' up to Frank Tucci's," said Johnny as he headed toward the door.

Joe grabbed a handful of black leather jacket. "Frank Tucci, the mobster?"

"No, Frank Tucci, the florist. Cleary put himself square in the middle of Gold and Tucci. All because of you." He yanked his jacket out of Quinlan's grip. "You're so busy trying to outrun the past, you don't know what's going on with the last two people in the world who care about you. Grow up, Quinlan. Heroes are the guys who put their lives on the line for somebody else, not bastards like you who are trying to prove how brave they are to an audience."

Johnny had hardly jerked open the door when he felt Quinlan's hand on his shoulder. "Get your hand off me," he said without turning around. "Or I'm going to gut you, no matter how big and mean you are."

"Wait for me, kid. I'm going with you."

Johnny looked over his shoulder. "Like hell you are."

"I owe Jack, kid, and this is my last chance to pay him back. I'm begging you to take me with you. I have to tell him something."

"What?"

"I have to tell him he did the right thing on that island during the war. For God's sake, kid, I've got to tell him thank you."

"Then let's go."

"Just a minute," said Quinlan, turning back to Eileen and grasping her shoulders. "I want to start a new life. I want it to be with you. Now what time does that bus leave?"

Johnny could see that Eileen didn't entirely believe Joe. He could understand that. Frankly he didn't quite believe him, either. But sometime or other, everybody deserves a second chance. "Nine-thirty," said Eileen, finally making up her mind.

"I'll be there," said Joe, kissing her forehead before turning back to Johnny. "Let's go kid."

Cleary skidded the Eldorado to a stop in front of Tucci's house, not worrying about whether the flying gravel would nick the Caddy's paint job. If it did, he would worry about it later. If there was a later. If he got blown away, then a few nicks wouldn't matter.

He pounded on the front door, and hoped whoever answered wouldn't shoot first and ask questions later. If that happened, it was going to be a real short visit. A second later, looking down the barrel of Ralphie's gun, he knew no bookie on the Strip would take bets

on his living long enough to blink his eyes. The book-
ies would be wrong, he thought as he slammed past
Ralphie and into the house. "I'm looking for Tucci."

Ralphie smiled. "Isn't that funny. He's been looking for you."

"You've got a great sense of humor, Ralphie," he
said as the hood patted him down and took his gun.
"Watch that. Loaded guns are dangerous."

Ralphie pushed him toward the stairs. "You're a
barrel of laughs yourself, Cleary. Mr. Tucci's waiting
to hear some more of your funny stories. But I gotta
warn you. He's not in a good mood this morning. He's
got a hair-trigger temper. His temper, my hairtrigger."
He laughed at his own joke more than Cleary thought
it was worth.

"Where's your kennelmate?" he asked as he
climbed the stairs.

"Keep up the smart remarks, Cleary, and I'll shoot
your kneecaps and tell Mr. Tucci it was an accident."

Cleary shut up. He was outgunned and out-
manned. Aggravating an already bad situation could
get him killed. On the other hand, it might not be
possible to aggravate Frank Tucci any more than he
already was. The crime lord came out of the shadows
like Dracula, a white towel around his neck, and
clearly looking for a victim. Dressed in a short silk
robe, last night's trousers, and a bandage as large as
Cleary's palm covering the right side of his neck,
Frank Tucci was angry.

"He packing heat?" Tucci asked Ralphie.

"A .38, but I got it. Maybe we can arrange for him
to eat it." Ralphie laughed again. Being shot at must
agree with him, thought Cleary. He seemed to find
everything so damn funny this morning.

Tucci moved to the bar and ran water on the towel,

then gently patted his face with it, studying Cleary as if he were a bug under a microscope. "This isn't a gangster movie, Cleary. You don't get any retakes. You and Gold missed your big chance," he finally said. "You got lousy shots out here in L.A. I wouldn't pay any hit men who emptied two submachine guns and didn't manage to kill anybody." His voice was loud, and straight from New York City's East Side.

"I was set up just like you, Tucci."

"You expect me to believe that? You think I got shit for brains?"

"You do if you believe I set you up, Tucci." He lowered his voice. "You think a hit man can pick and choose targets with a submachine gun like he could with a handgun? You've been in the business long enough to know better than that. No one was supposed to leave this room except in a body bag, me included. I had nothing to do with last night, and I'd be a damn fool to show up here by myself to finish the job. I'm here because I don't want to be looking over my shoulder waiting for one of those torpedoes to put a bullet in my back."

Tucci swiped at his ear with the wet towel and scrutinized Cleary, his black eyes revealing indecision. "You may be on the level, Cleary, and you may not. But before I decide what to do with you I'd like to know what your angle is."

"I told you: money," said Cleary, instinct telling him not to mention Joe's name. Never reveal a vulnerable spot to a viper like Tucci because that would be the next place he would bite. And Joe was a vulnerability, Cleary admitted to himself. He didn't know how much further he would go to protect a friend, and he didn't want to find out.

"Now you're lying, Cleary. The word on the Strip is that money doesn't mean much to you."

"Everybody needs money."

"Not Jack Cleary. Money won't buy you, certainly not the couple of grand Gold's paying. That's public opinion, and I've got no reason to disbelieve it. So the question is: what kind of a hold has Gold got on you? How'd a smart guy like you get involved in all this?"

Johnny parked the Merc at the bottom of the hill. "I'm walking from here. I don't want to risk setting anything off by roaring up to the house like gangbusters. You shake up a nest of hornets, and they're gonna sting everything in sight. I don't want Cleary to get stung. He'd get more than an itchy bump."

He slid out of the Merc and softly pushed the door shut. "Keep down and wait for the cops, Quinlan. Tell Fontana to keep the sirens off."

Joe slid out of the passenger side, a determined look on his face an opposing Roller Derby player would recognize. It said somebody was going to get knocked off the oval, and it wouldn't be Joe Quinlan. "I'm going with you."

"The hell you are, champ. You keeping your ass right down here where you're safe. I don't have time to worry about you taking off on your own again like you did when you made that deal with Gold."

Joe started up the hill. "Jack's in that hornets' nest because of me. The least I can do is risk getting stung, too. Besides, kid, you don't have time to argue with me, and you sure can't keep me down here unless you blast me or knock the hell out of me. I don't think you can do that. Cleary, maybe. He's had more practice telling himself it would be for my own good."

Johnny caught up with him. "All right, I'll let you come. But you obey orders, you hear?"

"You sound like the fucking army, kid," said Quinlan, a grin on his face.

Tucci's house came into view, a futuristic nightmare of circles, angles, and for all Johnny knew, square roots. All he knew for sure was that he didn't like it. It looked...cold. Like some kind of mausoleum out in Forest Lawn. It didn't look like any place he wanted to live. Or die. His shotgun dipped as he shivered. This was no time to think about dying. Damn it, Cleary, he thought. Why the hell did you have to get involved? Quinlan wasn't worth it, war buddy or not.

He glanced over at Quinlan. Cleary had saved his life, wiped his nose, picked up the pieces of his life and gave them back to him, and what had Quinlan done? Thrown the pieces down because they didn't look like they had before. Well, to hell with that. Everybody had to glue pieces of their lives back together, and the cracks always showed. But you slapped on the glue, stuck the chip back in where the hole was, and went on. Nothing came with a lifetime guarantee. Not even life.

Motioning Quinlan to follow, Johnny moved onto the lawn, running hunched over to the double car garage. The split-level house loomed over his head like something out of a science-fiction movie. He grasped the other man's shoulder. "You stay put. I'm going to check out the back, see if I can find a way in this place. You don't move, you hear me? Cleary wanted you safe, and I work for him, so I want you safe, too."

"Jack always spent too much time worrying about

keeping people safe. Most of the time he didn't bother to ask if that's what they wanted."

Quinlan's voice sounded strange, but Johnny didn't have time to analyze it. "If that's what Jack Cleary wants, it's good enough for me. You mess this up, and you'll find out I've had a lot of practice blasting people."

He moved off without another backward glance, sweat rolling down his sides, soaking the white T-shirt he wore under his leather jacket. It wasn't that hot, so he must be scared. He grinned to himself, felt his lips quiver, and tightened his mouth. Damn right he was scared. Cleary had stuck his neck out too far this time. Cleary's problem was that he was a real, honest-to-god hero and didn't know it. Johnny didn't have anything against heroes, except that there were more dead ones than live ones.

He noticed the boarded-up windows on the second story, and wondered what happened. Maybe everybody inside was dead. No, that didn't make sense. If everybody was dead, then who boarded up those windows? Climbing up a wall, he decided modern architecture wasn't so bad after all. All the odd angles and unnecessary walls made easy climbing.

Reaching the pool, he heard a voice screaming. Somebody's pissed, he thought. Then he heard another voice, Quinlan's voice! Son of a bitch was all he had time to think before he circled around the pool at a dead run looking for a way in.

Joe Quinlan stepped into Tucci's living room with his Army-issue .45 pointed at Tucci. "He's involved because of me."

"Who the hell are you?" demanded Tucci.

"His buddy," said Joe.

"He's gonna be nobody's buddy in a minute," said Ralphie, aiming his pistol square at Cleary's nose.

"Drop the gun!" said Joe.

"Take it easy, Joe. I've got everything under control here," interjected Cleary, seeing the anticipatory gleam in Ralphie's eyes, and the reckless look in Joe's.

"Like hell you do. These guys were gonna blow you away."

"Just say the word, Frank," said Ralphie.

"Tell him to put it down, Cleary," warned Tucci.

"Gimme the word, Frank," asked Ralphie again.

"Put the gun away, Joe," demanded Cleary, blinking away the sweat trickling into his eyes.

In that blink of an eye, that split second he couldn't see, his ears registered the first shot. He focused his stinging eyes, saw Joe stagger backward against the bar as two more shots punched obscene red holes in his chest. Mouth open, the dawning of a terrible knowledge in his eyes, Joe fell sprawling as his dying brain shut down motor functions to conserve energy to fuel consciousness until the last possible second.

"Joe!" screamed Cleary, and knocked the gun out of Ralphie's hand, then hammered him between the eyes, sending him crashing backward down the staircase.

"Cleary!" shouted Nico.

Cleary jerked his head up and saw Nico's still-smoking gun pointed at his heart. He was going to die. He knew it in his shrinking body, knew it and screamed a silent protest at dying uselessly at the hands of a man not good enough to be in the same room as Joe Quinlan. He froze—waiting, regretting, hating. There was no place to run, no choices to make.

The shotgun blast that released him and sent Nico Cero to hell left him weak as he staggered over to Joe. He barely noticed Tucci escaping through the shattered door, barely saw Johnny Betts loosely holding his shotgun, horror etched into his young face. He gently cradled Joe's head and shoulders in his arms, saw the radiating pain revealed in his friend's eyes.

Joe licked his lips, and took a shallow breath. "We got 'em, didn't we, Jack?"

Cleary examined Joe's wounds, saw the location of each, and knew the delicate organs that determined life and death of a body were damaged beyond a surgeon's skill. "You dumb son of a bitch. I had it under control. Why did you do it?"

Joe took several more shallow breaths, his eyes beginning to dull as the life began to flicker. "You were always there when I needed you." He laughed, and a spasm of pain twisted his mouth. "Even when I didn't want you to be. This time, it was my choice."

Cleary looked blindly around the room, caught a flash of Johnny's anguished face, saw a beefy cop push Tucci into the room at gunpoint, followed by Fontana come to collect his evidence against the forces of evil. Fontana abruptly stopped and holstered his .38. His face twisting with sympathy, he joined Johnny Betts in what Cleary knew was a deathwatch.

Cleary finally looked down at Joe again, suddenly angry, angry that life seemed to promise happy endings and delivered broken dreams instead. "Look at you," he said, his voice sounding hoarse. "What the hell happened to you?"

Joe smiled, his eyes blinking back the descending darkness. "Nothing happened to me. Everything changed after we got back. No call for heroes, Jack." He opened his eyes wide, as if he saw an essential truth he had deliberately avoided seeing. "Eileen didn't care about heroes. All she wanted me to do was catch a lousy bus. And I couldn't even do that."

His breath caught, then rushed past his lips in a moan, as if life blinked and then went out. Cleary clutched the empty shell that once was Joe Quinlan and looked up at Johnny Betts, and at Charlie Fontana, whose men walked quietly among the dead.

ELEVEN

Cleary saw the suitcases, stacked on the sidewalk in front of the house like the baggage of hopeless refugees he had seen during the war. He stopped the Eldorado and leaned his head against the steering wheel, willing the stinging tears to dry. Finally he raised his head and looked toward the house. Eileen must have been waiting just inside because she immediately stepped onto the porch, thick auburn hair glowing in the sun, large brown eyes looking hopefully toward him. Seeing the hope die was like seeing Joe die all over again.

"He's not coming back, is he, Jack?" she asked as he stopped by the edge of the porch.

He saw the grief beneath the ashes of hope and

knew words had to be said, and hoped he could find the right ones. "He wanted to, Eileen. He finally wanted to, but a hood named Cerro took away his chance." He stopped to get control of his voice. "He's dead, and I'm sorry. I tried to keep him out of it. I thought I could save him again. For what it's worth, he died trying to save my life," he finished bitterly.

He looked down at the cracked sidewalk, the flicks of blood on the front of his shirt, and felt guilty suddenly for being alive and talking to Joe's wife while he was still wearing a shirt covered with Joe's blood. He felt ashamed, as though he were a beggar asking for alms by exposing suppurating wounds on his body.

"It was his choice, Jack," said Eileen softly.

Cleary looked up to meet Eileen's eyes. They were filled with expressions of grief and a terrible acceptance. "What do you mean?"

She looked across the yard again, toward that vision only she could see. "He may have wanted to come back to me, but he wanted to be a hero again more. Maybe he thought he could do both. But when the time came he made the right choice."

He grabbed her shoulders. "You're talking crazy, Eileen. He loved you."

"But he couldn't live for me, could he, Jack? You can die for somebody, but you can't live for them. You've got to live for yourself. That's what he was doing when he saved your life. He was living for himself, he was being a hero, because that's all he ever was." She shook her head, splattering tears over her cheeks. "There just wasn't much room for Joe's kind of hero after the war." She placed her hands on top of his. "I'll arrange for the funeral, then I'm catching that bus. It's time for me to start living for myself, too."

He released her shoulders, watched her hands slide off his own, noticed how strong and capable they looked. "Is there anything I can do, Eileen?"

She looked at him and smiled. "Don't feel guilty."

"Give me something easy to do," he said bitterly.

"All right. Live for yourself. Go be your own kind of hero. Go find a dragon to slay even if it's only in your own mind."

"Those are easy?"

She shrugged, and looked old and bitter for a moment. "Heroes never make easy choices. If they did, they wouldn't be heroes, would they?"

He stepped on to the peeling tar-paper roof. There was no blaring radio, no thud of a baseball against the wall, no anguished man except himself. It was peaceful with the sunrise sound of birds and the gentle rush of wind. There were no ghosts here to whom he could apologize. Joe was gone, happy in his choice of graves. He had haunted this place when he was alive. There was no need to do so now.

He walked over to the ledge and picked up one of Joe's dirty, worn baseballs from the decaying basket. He stood, tossing the ball up in the air and catching it. Go slay a dragon Eileen had said. He looked over the rooftops, past the skyscrapers built since the war, to an old neighborhood of the city, a neighborhood whose residents believed in dragons. For five years he had avoided its streets, shunned its people, haunted its alleys and teahouses and gambling dens in his memories. Like Joe and his rooftop, he was a ghost in Chinatown.

He threw the ball away, backed up several steps, and with four quick strides launched himself into the air, felt its friction, tasted the acrid fear of death, and slammed into the ledge of the building opposite, clawing, grasping, finally pulling himself up. He straddled the ledge and looked down into the twelve-story chasm. "I'm alive," he said aloud. "I'm not a ghost, because ghosts don't slay dragons."

He slid off the ledge onto the roof and dusted off his hands. He touched the bail bondsman's commission in his breast pocket. Tonight he would go to Chinatown.

T W E L V E

Cleary took a deep breath. He could feel his heart pounding inside his chest as he knocked on the orange metal door with an embossed image of a dragon swallowing its own tail. That's what he had been doing for five years, swallowing his own tail. Eating himself up with guilt, or with a sense of failure. Maybe they were the same thing. Tonight he would confront himself, slay the dragon. If his mission in Chinatown was no heroic, life-or-death situation, it still gave him an opportunity. Maybe as he walked the familiar streets, he could forgive himself. Or find a way to pay a debt. If he did neither, then Joe Quinlan's death meant nothing. His dying wouldn't make a difference.

The sliding metal peephole opened, and two Chinese eyes peered out. "Jack Cleary," he said quietly, wondering if the name would still open doors in Chinatown.

The peephole closed and the still-silent Chinese swung open the door. Cleary stepped inside to be suddenly surrounded by masses of Chinese gamblers. Everything was a sensory attack. From the haze of incense that blurred the size of the narrow room, rendering indistinct the faces of excited men clustered around the gambling tables, to the auditory assault of high-pitched voices, the clacking of dominoes and mah-jongg tiles, chatter, cries, curses, and the monotonous singsong of numbers, bets, and losers, all in a language in which the emphasis of a single syllable could change the meaning of a word.

Anyone who claimed the Chinese were a silent, reserved, inscrutable race, had never been in a gambling den, thought Cleary, closing his eyes to breathe in the myriad odors. The air was filled with cigarette smoke, incense, and steam from the tea tables that sat off to one side. And the sweat of men in the close, hot night air of Chinatown. But seldom the cloying sweetness of opium. Opium served another function. It had no place in a gambling hall where the object was another kind of nirvana: that of winning. With his eyes closed he could feel the excitement and tension as a palpable thing, composed of the desperation of men needing to win almost as much as they needed to eat.

He opened his eyes, blinking away the prickling caused by the incense, and looked at the men. To many of them, to win was to eat. The laborers, paid less than their labor was worth, the deliverymen, waiters, noodle makers, fish butchers still splashed with blood and scales, men in aprons and men in three-piece suits, all in unblinking concentration upon the next throw of the dice or tiles or dominoes. There were powerfully built men with rags tied around their heads, now wet with sweat, and old fragile men dressed in traditional Chinese clothes, who bet with care and precision. But all had in common the black oblique eyes and yellowed ivory skin of the Oriental. Only Cleary was unique in this world, with his white skin and round blue eyes.

But no one spared him a glance. He had passed through the orange door with its embossed dragon. He must belong. And there were other more important men to worry about, men whose words meant the difference between a bowl of rice or an empty belly for those who gambled what they could not afford. The pit bosses, one at each table, were the gods of this den. They somehow, by the grace of Heaven, kept track of the furious betting, raking in hundreds at a time, wagered and lost in a matter of seconds. Their low, steady monotones of confidence were in contrast to the high-pitched betting. Their black eyes flickered with the quickness of fireflies around the table, missing nothing, cataloging all with the precision of a machine.

Cleary scrutinized the faces in the room, but the shapes wavered and shifted in the cloud of incense, and it was impossible to be certain of an identity. Accepting that fact with the fatalism of the Chinese, he weaved through the maze of tables, feeling the tension grow as the night aged and laborers held off losing their money as long as they could. But eventually they would rise, broke but no wiser, ready to chase the vision again the next week. For most of them, Cleary knew, it was the only way out of the world of

Chinatown. And most wouldn't make it. Couldn't, in many cases. They were locked into its alleys and streets by traditions stronger than any prison bars.

He claimed an empty chair at the fan-tan table, sliding into it with a sense of coming home. The flashing neon signs threw colored lights across his hands and the faces of the other players. He knew if he turned around and glanced out the long, low window behind him, he would see those same neon signs reflecting intense primary colors off the wet, rainy streets of Chinatown—red and yellow of the flashing signs of restaurants and bars, their colors splashing off the street to highlight the curved rooflines of the pagoda buildings.

He bet furiously with the other gamblers, his Chinese only faintly accented. Raking in his winnings, he searched the room like a casual Occidental visitor, curious to gawk at the slant-eyed foreigners. It was a good cover, because if white men found Oriental faces impossible to read, the reverse was also true. Cleary knew that to ninety-nine percent of the Chinese in this room, he was an inscrutable foreign devil, possibly evil, certainly uncivilized and barbaric, just barely above the level of a dog in the scheme of things. He could live with that.

Peering across the incense-clouded room, he saw his prey. He knew that to the average person, there was nothing distinctive about this particular Chinese. The man was just another faceless laborer, filthy from his job somewhere in the bowels of Chinatown. But Cleary knew the average person could not tell one Chinese from another. But he didn't have that problem. Other than sharing the same hair and eye color, and even that varied, the Chinese were as different from one another as Chinatown and old Los

Angeles. They weren't stamped out with a cookie cutter like most whites thought.

Easing out of his chair and moving down the room, past the long, low window, Cleary never took his eyes off the Chinese. What he was about to do was not as dangerous as most people would think. The Chinese had an ingrained, almost instinctive respect for authority. And he was authority, at least of a sort.

"Been a long time, Cleary," said an accented voice, slurring over the *l* in his name.

The Chinese had a difficult time pronouncing that particular English sound, thought Cleary, wiping his face of any expression as he turned toward the tong boss man. "Not by the look of things, it hasn't," he said, managing an easy smile and gesturing toward the rest of the room.

With a half smile, the boss man stepped down from the counting room that sat above the gambling table at the end of the room. Before the door closed, Cleary saw a couple of counters thumbing through stacks of money with incredible speed. "Business is good, I see."

The boss man gave him another half smile. "Some days it is good; some days it is bad. Today it is good." He nodded toward a table crowded with laborers. "It is like opium to some."

"Then why don't you keep them out?" asked Cleary, and immediately regretted his comment. In Chinatown, it was rude to criticize your host.

The boss man's smile disappeared. "Then they would go outside to gamble, and that would not do."

Cleary knew that outside meant the rest of the city, or the rest of the world for that matter. The tong wanted no part of the outside world, and L.A.'s homegrown gangsters wanted no part of any exotic imports. Crime lords had their prejudices just like the rest of the population.

"I understand," he finally said. And he did, too. It was a matter of power. The various tongs held what amounted to absolute power over the residents of Chinatown. If the price of that power was a few laborers gambling away their wages and ending up begging in the gutters, so be it. It was the order of things. And that was something else Cleary understood about the Chinese. They held life cheap, and they were conservative to the point of idiocy. Change wasn't one of the race's favorite vocabulary words.

"Enjoy the games, Cleary," said the boss man, smiling again now that the foreign devil acknowledged the order of things.

Cleary nodded. "Some other time. I have business here." It was best to announce up front that he had a job to do, and that it had nothing to do with gambling. That, too, was the order of things.

The boss man's eyes flitted about the room, finally settling on the Chinese laborer. "We have been expecting someone. We did not know it would be you. It is well." He inclined his head in a gesture of respect. Cleary, after all, was not one of them.

Cleary dipped his head back. While the tong would not deliberately turn over one of their own to the foreign devil's law, they would not interfere, either. The Chinese laborer was a man with no power, and he had ventured outside, had broken the strange laws of the foreign devils, had brought unwelcome attention to Chinatown. He had disturbed the order of things. He would be sacrificed.

The boss man continued cruising through the room, giving instructions in a low, confident voice. Cleary knew none of those instructions concerned him. His job was an unpleasantness to be ignored. He shrugged his shoulders and moved over to the mah-jongg table. Action was in high gear, betting at one hundred miles an hour, tiles clicking against one another like a race car's wheels on an uneven road.

He finally stood next to the Chinese laborer who was betting with great intensity, a quiet desperation that told Cleary the game was more important than life. The laborer didn't notice Cleary until he reached out his hand to place a bet with the mah-jongg tile. He couldn't miss the handcuff that the foreigner expertly slapped on his wrist. He was so stunned he froze, his hand still reaching out with his bet. He looked up at Cleary with an expression of horror, his face turning as white as someone's with yellow skin could turn.

"Don't look so surprised, friend. When you jump bail in this town, they send someone. Even down here," Cleary said, as with a sure and permanent click, he slapped the other end of the handcuffs on his own wrist.

The look on the laborer's face was one of disbelief, mixed with that profound resignation at missing out on his pot of gold at the end of the rainbow. Cleary ground his teeth in irritation. Damn Chinese fatalism, anyway. They shouldn't be so goddamn accepting. The guy was so sure fate was against him he didn't even notice that he had won the money sitting on the table.

Cleary nudged him. "Go ahead, pick up your dough. The rest of your night looks like a washout, but that's no reason not to grab what you've already won. Go on, do a little living for yourself." He smiled at hearing himself repeat Eileen's words.

The laborer reached for his money, his eyes still

expressing disbelief, when the secured orange doors burst open. Two bandits wearing Chinese masks, one waving a two-inch .38, and the other holding a sawed-off shotgun, pushed the two "look see boys" into the room. Now everyone's eyes held disbelief as the room fell silent in waves, the gamblers in front falling back in the face of the ugly guns.

One man covered the gamblers as the other rushed into the counting room and threw the counters out, then shoveled the money into a sack as fast as he could. The two moved fast, without a word spoken. They're pros, thought Cleary, and they know what they want. He watched them sweep through the room like an evil wind, raking the money off the tables into the bag. The boss man wouldn't be happy. It wasn't going to be such a good night after all.

Looking up, he noticed a couple of tong gunmen ease their hands to their concealed guns, but the bandit with the shotgun casually pointed his weapon at the two men. The Chinese shrugged and dropped their hands. So be it. It was the order of things.

Cleary tried to fade into the background. Which was going to be tough since he was the only white man in the joint. Very carefully, he placed the key to the cuffs in the slot and began to turn it. Something bad could happen very soon, *would* probably happen, and the last thing he needed was to be cuffed to a Chinese. Freedom of movement was necessary if a guy had to run like hell for the door.

Feeling tension increase around the table, and hearing the laborer cuffed to him suck in his breath, Cleary looked up. He hadn't been quite fast enough. The bandit with the shotgun had noticed him. Avoiding looking up, he tried to blend in with the furniture. Which wasn't very successful, either, since he didn't

look any more like the furniture than he looked Chinese. Giving up, he met the bandit's eyes and caught
a spark of recognition. The bandit might remember
him from Cleary's days on the Chinatown beat when
he was a cop, or maybe the bandit was just happy
because he found somebody he would like to blow up
because he was white. It was a good bet either way.

Despite the fact he was in a big hurry, the bandit
took the time to come up to stand mask to nose with
Cleary. Locking his eyes with Cleary's, the bandit
tapped the handcuffs with the shotgun barrel to see if
the two men were actually locked together. The mask
moved imperceptibly as if the man underneath had
smiled. Cleary was glad the thug found something
funny about the situation because he sure as hell
hadn't.

He watched the twelve-gauge barrel move slowly
and steadily until it rested against his neck. It was
cold and uncomfortable, and he had an aversion to
gun barrels parked against his neck. Just a personal
quirk of his. He had an aversion to being searched,
too, which was what the bandit was doing with his
other hand. And he damn sure had an aversion to
having some low-life scum take his winnings and his
watch. On the other hand, he wouldn't bet on his
chances of knocking the gun away and hammering
the bandit, not with a Chinese cuffed to him. He
might as well practice a little fatalism of his own.
When you can't fight them, stand still.

He gritted his teeth when the bandit found his .38
with the two-inch barrel. So much for his ace in the
hole, or mah-jongg tile on the table, as the case may
be. His mouth dropped open when the thug placed
the .38 in his hand, backed up three or four steps,
then turned his back and slowly walked away. His

fingers tightened around the grip and he rested his
finger against the trigger. The son of a bitch was dar-
ing him to fire.

Cleary took a deep breath, then another, and held
it. He slowly moved the gun an inch at a time,
squeezing the trigger a little tighter with each inch.
With luck, he could get off a clean shot, then dive for
the floor and shoot the other hood on the way down.
He watched the bandit intently and realized luck
wasn't with him. For every inch he moved his gun,
the bandit turned his muzzle back toward him. For
relative size, a shotgun muzzle had it all over a .38.
Besides, at this distance the bandit didn't need a
clean shot. Any kind of a shot would take off various
head and body parts of Jack Cleary, as well as those of
anybody who didn't duck fast.

He let his breath out a little at a time, and eased
his finger off the trigger. Gently, moving slowly, he
lowered his hand and placed the .38 on the gambling
table. He heard a *whoosh* of relief as the others
around him expelled their pent-up breaths. Amazing
how everybody holds their breath when they're
scared to death, he thought.

The bandit shrugged slightly, and walking back,
swept the money off the gambling table, including
the winnings of the Chinese laborer. In his hurry to
stuff the money into the bag, the bandit spilled some
of it on the floor. Cleary heard his handcuffed partner
catch his breath, and nudged him. Now was not the
time to disturb the order of things. Now was the time
to be a typical, inscrutable, *fatalistic* Chinese. It beat
being a dead Chinese.

The two bandits backed up to the orange door, still
covering the room, and Cleary reached slowly for the
key which was still in the handcuffs, never taking his

eyes off the two men. He noticed the laborer was staring at the money lying at his feet as though his eyes were riveted to it. Just as the bandits backed through the door, the Chinese lunged for the money.

"No!" screamed Cleary, but the sound was lost in the blast of the shotgun as the bandit caught the laborer's movement out of the corner of his eye and whirled around, unloading both barrels into the Chinese.

"Jesus, God!" Cleary gasped as the laborer was blown backward, yanking Cleary with him. They hit the table and slid onto the floor in the midst of hell breaking loose as the other gamblers scrambled away in panic. He gazed into eyes blinded to any consideration but that of staying alive, and staying alive meant getting away from the foreign devil and the crazy Chinese. He couldn't blame them. Nobody wants to stay in the vicinity of a shotgun target.

Blinking to clear his eyes, he focused on his torn and bleeding companion. Lights seemed to flicker as he thought for a minute he was looking at Joe Quinlan. It was too damn much, he wanted to scream. Less than twenty-four hours ago, only this morning, he had held another corpse in his arms. Now this. And both of them didn't have any damn business getting killed. He couldn't take much more of this, or he would be puking his guts out in some alley, just one more guy hiding in a bottle.

He clenched his shaking hand. No, he wouldn't, by God. A guy can't kill a dragon from inside a whiskey bottle, and he was going to slay those two if it was the last thing he did. Taking a deep breath, he quickly snapped off the now unlocked cuffs and, snatching his .38, turned and leveled it at the two bandits. Damn it, he thought. In the pandemonium, there was no way to get off a clear shot without risking some other innocent, dirt-poor, scared Chinese.

He watched, feeling his hot breath whistle between his lips as the bandits disappeared, then raced over to the door, delivered a kick in the middle of the embossed dragon's belly that left the door swinging from a busted hinge, and lunged into the hallway. He stumbled a step to look down the stairs just as the second bandit unleashed both barrels again and blasted the wall inches from his head.

"Goddamn it!" he spat, hitting the worn, dusty hall carpet on his belly. His breath left him in a rush, and he gasped for air. Fortunately he had always been able to walk and chew gum at the same time, so he was able to get off several shots at the same time he was persuading his body to breathe again.

The two bandits burst out the street-level door, and Cleary scrambled after them, his weary body breathing again but protesting with every breath. He burst through the door himself, gun level, to find—nothing. The maze of streets that was Chinatown had already swallowed up the bandits.

THIRTEEN

Cleary leaned against the window studying the now transformed gambling den. It might have been any narrow, stark, empty room, cluttered with a few toppled mah-jongg tables, strewn gambling paraphernalia, and a dead man on the floor. There was a lingering odor of incense and sweat, Chinese tea, and the humid air of Chinatown. Violence didn't leave behind a smell unless you counted the sweetish scent of human blood.

He smoked a cigarette and stared down at the dead Chinese laborer at his feet. The neon lights flashed through the long window at his back and threw bars of red and yellow across each of them. The colors were appropriate; red for blood, and yellow for the

laborer's ivory skin, now lifeless and shrunken looking. Amazing how quickly a human being shrank
after death, he thought, shuffling the two cigarette
butts away from the corpse. It was as if life had some
kind of substance, and once it was gone, the corpse
collapsed inward. He glanced at his watch and wondered how much longer he had to keep company with
a dead man. It had already been too long.

He shivered and rubbed his arms. He had placed
his coat over the Chinese's face and chest, and now
he was cold. But not as cold as the corpse, he
thought, observing the pool of blood that had coagu-
lated under the coat. Nothing would warm him again.

He glanced back at the window, at the wet streets
and neon signs, the pagodas and bars. There were no
people, as there should be at night. The word had
seeped into the streets and alleys, bars and teahouses,
brothels and shops. A man was murdered in Chinatown; the white police would be coming. Stay in, stay
silent, stay blind. The tong has spoken. When night
descends again, we will come, we will question, we
will know. That is the order of things.

Cleary ground out his cigarette, crouched down,
and examined the dead man closely. He was just a
laborer, not worth much in this society, or most others
for that matter. A thousand more would take his place
tomorrow, and he would end up in the morgue with a
cardboard tag tied to his toe while the pathologist cut
him up. His luck had been bad in more ways than
one tonight. He lost his winnings and lost his life, but
more than that, he would go to his grave mutilated, a
sure way for a Chinese to miss out on any kind of
hereafter.

Cleary looked more closely at the man. His closed
eyes and forehead, above the coat that covered his

face and chest, looked peaceful. The forehead was high and slightly domed, the features were delicate and intelligent, rather than coarse and flat. He looked more mandarin than laborer. Cleary respectfully removed his handcuffs from the dead man's wrist, noticing as he did that the Chinese's hand was long and slender, like a pianist's. Turning over the hand, he checked out the palm. There were calluses, but new ones. Whoever the man was, other than a bail jumper, he had come down from his place in the world. Cleary wondered how that had happened. Chinese society was rigid. A man born to an intellectual life seldom lost his place.

Standing up, he put the cuffs back into his pocket. Joe Quinlan and now this Chinese. Both of them more than they seemed to be, and both of them dead. No connection between the two except a tired, sickened private eye named Jack Cleary.

He heard the street-level door open and two men, talking and joking, climbing the stairs. He recognized the voices, and felt even sicker. Of all the plainclothes detectives on the LAPD, why did it have to be Sfakis and Hine? He had taken about all he could stand today. He wasn't sure he could take those two assholes.

They entered the room together, each holding fortune cookies, and each chewing on toothpicks, like a couple of macabre Bobbsey Twins. Except they didn't look like twins at all. Hine was well oiled, with short curly hair turning gray, and handsome looks dissipated by overindulgences. Sfakis had a Detroit flattop, so short the scalp showed through, and no neck. His head sat directly on his shoulders like Humpty-Dumpty. Cleary always wondered why Sfakis bothered to buy ties. He might as well paint a knot on his chin and stripes down his shirtfront and let it go at that.

The two detectives glanced at Cleary, but not at the Chinese. He was just a clod of mud not worth noticing until it was time to sweep it up. Sfakis pointed a thick finger at one particular fortune cookie in Hine's big hand. "I gotta feeling about this one."

Hine looked at Cleary. "Every day we eat Chinese, and every freakin' day I got to read him his fortune." He snapped open the cookie and pulled out the strip of paper. "'You will find fame and fortune in Chinatown.' Feel better now?"

Sfakis put his arm around his partner's shoulders and smiled. It was enough to make Cleary sicker than he already was. "Much." He looked at Cleary. "Kinda like you, huh, Cleary? You got pretty famous down here, didn't ya? They still talk about you in the teahouses. Anybody would think you were just another Chink."

Cleary shot him a look.

"Oh, our man's a little pissed," said Sfakis, nudging Hine. "He don't like to be called a Chink. He just likes to sleep with them."

Cleary shot over, wrapped Sfakis's tie around his fist, and jerked until the detective's face was almost touching his. "You're down here to investigate a murder, not rag my ass."

Hine grabbed Cleary from behind and pulled him off. "Pull that again, Cleary, and you can go downtown and spend the night in a cell full of hoods, and I'll make sure I tell them you used to be a cop."

Cleary jerked out of Hine's grip, not too difficult considering how drunk the detective was. "You keep him off my back."

Sfakis straightened his tie, his eyes hard and cold.

"I'll remember this, Cleary. You try anything funny again, and I'll charge you with assaulting a police officer."

The sick, cold feeling in Cleary's belly increased. It always did when he had done something stupid, and even touching Sfakis was stupid. All he had done had been to give the scum some leverage. "You gonna check out the scene or not?"

Hine bent down and pulled back Cleary's coat. He looked at the body as if it were road kill, and not very desirable road kill at that. "That's one seriously dead Chinaman. You happy now, Cleary?"

Cleary tightened his jaw. "Hardly worth interrupting your supper, huh, Hine? Although I guess it didn't spoil your appetite," he added, watching Sfakis chomping on fortune cookies like an inferior breed of bull.

Hine dropped the coat, making sure it landed in the sticky pool of blood. "Go to hell, Cleary."

Sfakis swallowed his cookie. "Hey, this isn't even our call, Cleary. We were gang-banging spareribs down the street when we heard the squeal. You better cool it down."

Cleary started to answer, but heard more footsteps coming up the stairs. These were heavy footfalls of tired, reluctant men who grunted all the way up to the room.

"Here comes Itch and Scratch," said Hine, going over to lean against the window frame and pick his teeth.

Cleary nearly groaned. Sfakis and Hine were bad enough, but at least they knew which way was up in Chinatown. Itch and Scratch, or Owens and Natell, were barely able to zip their sagging pants in the morning. He looked toward the door as two cops in uniform tromped into the room, big-bellied lifers, patrol cops, pulling up those same sagging pants and adjusting their guns. They had been playing good-cop, bad-cop for so long on the streets that they had adopted those faces as their own. Owens was the smiling, good-natured guy, and Natell the sourpuss with a face that would curdle milk. They were both equally dumb.

"That must be the first time either of you two flatfoots had to climb a stair in Chinatown," said Hine.

"Came as soon as we could, *Detective*," said Owens, his cheerful, good-natured face tightening up with sour lines.

Natell looked around the empty room. "They said this was supposed to be a gambling den. This don't look like no gambling den to me."

Cleary exchanged a look with Sfakis and Hine. He had more in common with the two detectives than he did with the two flatfoots who didn't have a clue as to what was going on in Chinatown. "You expected roulette wheels and opium pipes, Natell?"

"It's only been their beat since the freakin' war," said Hine. "They still need a city map to find the place."

Owens held on to his good humor and ignored the crack. Besides, Cleary figured it was true. "Ya get a good look at the guy?"

Cleary sighed. Evidently Owens and Natell were all the department was going to send. "There were two. Wearing some kind of Chinese clown masks."

Sfakis waded in with his comments which, as usual, left a lot to be desired as far as Cleary was concerned. "That's it? Clown masks? That's all you got?"

"I was too busy trying to keep from being blasted

across the room to ask to see their driver's licenses, Sfakis. And they sure as hell didn't volunteer any information. You guys are the cops! It's your job to investigate. You got a dead man lying here, for Christ's sake!"

"Knowing Cleary, I'm not surprised," said Natell under his breath, but just loud enough to be heard.

That was it! Enough! More than enough, thought Cleary, tired and angry. Grabbing Natell, he slammed him against the wall. "You talking to me, Natell?"

"You got a curse, private eye? Anybody gets too tight with you, they get blown away. You already had one guy stiffed today. You trying to set a record?"

Grief slammed him in the chest, leaving him panting. "You calling me a murderer?" demanded Cleary, wanting to sink his fist into Natell's beer belly.

"No! But you sure attract them. If Jack Cleary's around, sooner or later there's gonna be a stiff. You're trouble. Always have been."

"Shut up, Natell. If you boys in blue did your job instead of standing around cadging free beer off the bartenders, there wouldn't be any cesspools in this city, and no need for anybody to hire a private eye to clean them out."

Owens grabbed Cleary's arm. "Hey, that's my partner you're talking to," he began.

"No! I thought he rented that uniform from a costume shop."

Natell pushed himself away from the wall, his sour face looking as if it had been drenched in vinegar and hung out to dry. "You're pushing, Cleary. You always did, even when you were a cop. 'Gotta make a difference,' was your motto. You never could see that some things never change. Like Chinatown. We make about as much difference as a flea on a dog's ass."

"Natell, Owens!"

Cleary looked up to see Charlie Fontana enter the room followed by two SID men, two uniformed cops who appeared to have enough sense to hit the urinal in the men's room, and a couple of grunts from Central Receiving.

"Why don't you two boys make yourself useful and dust the stairwell or something," continued Fontana, rubbing his hands over his tired, lined face. This was Fontana's second homicide of the day, too, remembered Cleary.

Owens and Natell traded disgruntled looks, then headed out the door with the same slow, heavy steps with which they entered. The SID men went to work with fingerprint powder, cameras, tape measures, and all the other paraphernalia of crime detection. The scene would be printed, photographed, measured, swept, scraped, classified, and filed in a manilla folder after being reduced to typed reports. It was all very scientific, very efficient, very cold; a human tragedy reduced to statistics to be used in the next city budget meeting. Cleary hated it, hated the impersonality of an investigation. By the time the case got to court, if it even did, nothing was human anymore. Not even the corpse.

Fontana strolled over to Cleary, and turned around to study the room. "I came over soon as I heard, Jack," he said in a low voice. "It's been a hell of a day for you. Why did you have to come to Chinatown tonight? Couldn't you have at least waited until Quinlan was buried, give yourself some rest time? You need more business in Chinatown like L.A. needs more smog."

"I had a job to do," Cleary said, watching the

grunts as they lifted the body onto the meatwagon cart. "Besides, I had to slay a dragon."

Fontana looked at him for a long moment. "Looks like it's going to slay you. Do me a favor and get out of Chinatown. You can't turn back the clock. Like Natell said, you came down here to push. Well, give it up, Jack. You can't change anything in Chinatown. You can't change the tong. The dragon will swallow you up."

Cleary looked at Fontana, his eyes burning and his mind raw with the horror of the day. "I didn't know you were poetical, Charlie."

Fontana's face went cold and still as he became a cop talking to a civilian. "Keep your nose clean while you're down here, Jack. I don't want any trouble, and I don't want to get a call to pick up a stiff in some back alley and find out it's you."

"You won't, I promise."

Fontana looked at him as though he didn't believe him, then walked over to the body. He gently lifted Cleary's coat off the body and looked at the dead man. Cleary saw the weary resignation in his eyes, the kind that comes with the experience of years of homicides. Fontana had seen too many corpses killed in too many places and in too many different ways to be anything but resigned. A cop couldn't get indignant over every murder. They handled too many. Private eyes, on the other hand, could afford to get involved and be indignant.

Fontana nodded to the two men, and they wheeled the body out, leaving only a chalked outline and a large puddle of blood behind. He handed Cleary his coat. "Give me a minute and get SID started, then we'll take it over to Frank Tang's."

"Hey, what do you say, Cleary? It'll be just like old times," said Hine.

Cleary stood looking at the chalk outline of the laborer with the pianist's hands and the intellectual face. He didn't want that man's murderer to walk. He didn't want the case shoved into Pending because it was just another Chinese. "Not if I can help it," he said, ignoring Fontana's suddenly worried look.

F O U R T E E N

Some things certainly never changed in Chinatown, thought Cleary, and Frank Tang's Restaurant
and Bar was one of those things. A curtain of red
glass beads still separated the bar from the restaurant
area, and a waiter glided through it with a tray of hors
d'oeuvres and a lingering exotic tinkle. Only in Chinatown could cheap glass beads sound exotic. Anywhere else in the city, they would be thrown in the
trash.

He swirled the liquor around in his glass and listened to the other noises that weren't so exotic: the
muffled hum of conversation and occasional boisterous laughter from his companions, mixed with the
satiny strains of "Good Night My Love," playing on

the wood veneer Magnavox behind the bar. It was Frank Tang's; it was home.

He turned around and watched the Chinese waiters placing the stools upside down on the tables, but quietly, so as not to disturb the quiet ambience of the room. Other waiters, their Oriental faces placid masks, stood around, wanting to go home, but attentive to the needs of the cops. This was the foreign devils' hangout when they came to Chinatown, and it would not do to antagonize them. It would disturb the order of things.

He twisted around on a bar stool and observed his company for the night. Hine and Sfakis, as well as Fontana, had made themselves comfortable around the bar, spreading out as if they owned the place. He wasn't surprised at Hine and Sfakis. They were barbarians anyway, treating Frank and his help like Chinese coolies, but he was disappointed in Charlie Fontana. His old partner was listening to Hine and Sfakis's line of biased malarkey as if it were engraved on tablets and handed down from on high.

Frank Tang stood behind the bar smoothly distributing drinks all around. Hine and Sfakis continued talking as if Tang and the other Chinese didn't exist. They were both real sensitive.

"I just hope to hell we're not headed for another tong war down here. These people kill like machines. Life just don't mean nothing to them," said Hine, grabbing an egg roll off the hors d'oeuvre tray.

Sfakis shrugged his shoulders. Cleary noticed his head shrugged, too. That was what happened when you didn't have a neck. "That's fine by me." He grinned. "Long as they keep it in the 'Famiry.'"

Cleary shot Sfakis a look. The cop stared back puzzled. That figured, thought Cleary. Sfakis was so stupid he couldn't even recognize when someone looked at him like they would look at something stuck to the bottom of their shoe.

Frank Tang sat a fresh drink in front of Cleary. "Bourbon and soda—with a twist." He was second or third generation Chinese, Cleary didn't remember which, but his voice still had a slight accent.

With a flourish, Tang rubbed the sliver of lemon peel around the rim, and Cleary was caught off-guard by the little ritual. It brought back a lot of memories, some he didn't want to remember. Tang gave him a little smile, and he nodded back in appreciation. His eyes stung from fatigue, and maybe a tear. After all this time, Frank Tang remembered.

He watched the bar owner move off as Fontana touched his shoulder. "What the hell were you doing up there anyway, Jack? What kind of job did you take that left you standing guard over a dead Chinaman?"

Cleary rubbed the back of his neck where a painful stiffness was demanding attention. "The guy had jumped bail on some penny-ante grocery theft. I was hired to bring him in, save the bondsman his two hundred bucks," he finished bitterly.

"I wondered what your excuse for coming back was, Jack," said Fontana, his face sober. "I remember that case. It's not worth the court costs. If you hadn't taken the job, the bail bondsman would have written off his loss next week, and forgotten it by the week after that."

"The poor Chinese got written off instead," said Cleary, feeling his features tighten.

"I don't know why you're giving yourself such a rash about one lousy Chinaman, Cleary," said Hine, licking sauce off his fingers.

"The man's dead, Hine. Somebody shot him. Doesn't that mean anything to you?"

Sfakis leaned around his partner to look down the bar at Cleary. "You ain't been down here in a while, Cleary. Maybe you forgot. Nobody dies in Chinatown."

"That's right, Cleary," chimed in Hine. "Some other Chink just off the boat will have his identity by tomorrow morning. The tong just puts the guy's apron on someone else, and bingo, a miracle."

Sfakis grinned. "Kinda like the resurrection." He reached for another egg roll, dipped it in mustard sauce, and popped it into his mouth, followed by a large swallow of water. Chinese mustard was hot as hell, and Cleary wished he could force-feed the whole bowl to the fat slob.

Cleary put down his drink. "And all you two are going to do is sit right here drinking booze on the cuff."

Hine snickered, weaving slightly on the bar stool, his eyes red veined and glazed. "That's right, man. Just as long as Frankie Tang will serve it. And that better be as long as I want it," he added, an ugly note in his voice. "Hey, Tang," he called, his words slurring. "Give us another round. We're defending law and order in Chinatown, and it's thirsty work."

Tang had anticipated the demand, and was already heading their way with another tray of drinks. Cleary saw the bourbon and soda with the sliver of lemon peel, and suddenly swallowed back bile. His drink on the same tray as the drinks for Hine and Sfakis, like he was one of them. He swallowed again and rose, reaching into his pocket and extracting a few bills.

"Where are you going, Jack?" asked Fontana, his

eyes sunken with fatigue and disillusionment. The hope was buried deep tonight, almost too deep to see.

"While these guys are busy belly-bumping their way toward a pension"—he dropped the money on the table, glanced at the three cops—"I'm going to look into this. This guy isn't going to just lose his name to somebody else. This time somebody really did die in Chinatown. And I'm going to find out why."

"What's the big deal here, Cleary? It was just one Chinaman robbing another Chinaman and a third Chinaman got killed."

Cleary didn't dignify Hine's remark by answering, but finished his drink, waved away Frank Tang's offer of the fresh one, and started for the door. "See ya, Charlie."

"You remember what I said, Jack," Fontana said. "Don't push."

Cleary nodded to Tang as he passed. The Chinese proprietor was the only civilized man in the house, himself included.

"Hey, Cleary," Sfakis yelled after him. "You still chasing ghosts?"

He didn't dignify that comment with a reply, either. There was no point in trying to explain what he wasn't sure he understood himself. He had come to Chinatown to bury a ghost, and now there were two ghosts. Both Chinese, both innocent, both swept away in the gutter like so much trash. If he could avenge the laborer's death, maybe it would balance the scales, and the other ghost would give him some peace.

He walked, his mind a blank, until the soft light of dawn picked out details of Chinatown. The street was deserted, a couple of slow-moving vegetable trucks and an occasional work-weary Chinese coming off an all-night shift were the only signs of life. A Chinese noticed his Caucasian face and ducked his head. A white man in Chinatown at dawn could only mean trouble.

Cleary passed storefronts with catfish lying in shallow boxes of ice, melting on the sidewalk, stacks of exotic vegetables on the pavement in front of the closed shops. It was foreign, it was familiar, it was part of his past; a door he had never closed. He had to close it this time, stop the leaks of past into present, or he would be trapped worse than a convict in a prison of his own making. He had to restore the order of things in his own world, and he could do it only by changing this one. So be it.

He stopped and shook a cigarette out of his pack. As he flicked open his lighter and lit up, he looked up at a familiar street sign marking the intersection of Hill and Flower streets, the one place he didn't want to be, not tonight, not ever. Like the streets, her life and his had intersected only once.

Light and time seemed to blur, surroundings to lose color. He saw her on the other side of the street, her large, almond-shaped eyes looking at him with fear and hopelessness and wanting. The wind molded the red satin dress against her slender body and ruffled the silky curtain of black hair. He caught a faint odor of jasmine and lifted his hand. The sun rose over the buildings, caught her in its spotlight, and she vanished like mist, leaving behind—nothing.

He blinked, his hand and arm frozen in a motion of reaching out to touch what wasn't there. He staggered across the street, his legs moving in slow motion like sluggish, hung-over winos in the morning light. He reached the spot where he had seen her, searched the alleys on either side of the block, peered through locked shop windows. Finally he sank down on the sidewalk, resting his head on his bent knees. She was there; he saw her, saw her dress blow in the wind, even smelled her perfume. Raising his head, he looked back across the street at a limp banner, lettered in Chinese and hung from a second-story window. He covered his face with his hands, felt the stubble that reminded him he hadn't shaved in three days, and wondered if he was completely crazy. He couldn't have seen her, couldn't have traced the shape of her breasts when the wind flattened her high-collared Chinese tunic against her body, couldn't have smelled her perfume. There was no wind this morning. The air was absolutely motionless, as if it, too, was holding its breath waiting to see Jack Cleary shatter into more pieces than an exploded firecracker.

He pushed himself up, heard bones pop in protest, and swayed dizzily as he straightened. Not enough sleep. That was what was wrong. He hadn't slept in a couple of days, and he was disoriented. He had read somewhere that lack of sleep caused hallucinations. The alternative, that he was really seeing ghosts, was impossible. But in case it wasn't, he was going to exorcise that particular ghost. It was either that, or Fontana might really find him in an alley somewhere, not dead, but a blithering idiot.

Looking up and down the street, he spotted a phone booth and stumbled toward it. Reaching it, he rested his head against one of its glass walls for a second, taking deep breaths until he stopped shaking. He raised his head and looked back toward the place where she had materialized. "It's not going to happen again. I'm not going to let it," he called to the empty street. "It's going to be different this time. I'm going to make it different."

A Chinese shopkeeper unlocked his shop door and looked curiously at Cleary, then went back inside and dropped the shutter over his door again. Foreign devils meant trouble, but crazy foreign devils were worse.

Cleary reached in his pocket for a coin and inserted it into the telephone. Dialing his office number, he gently pressed his thumb against his closed eyelids, hoping to relieve the dry, burning sensation, while he listened to the phone ring.

"Just a minute," answered a voice on the other end. Cleary heard the receiver thud against something as Johnny Betts dropped it.

"Damn it to hell!" Johnny's exasperated voice came out of the receiver, then the sound of paper products being crushed, then more cursing. "Tomato beef chow mein all over my T-shirt. Stuff tasted like garbage anyway. Probably canned in Iowa." The Everly Brothers singing "All I Have to Do Is Dream" served as background music to his grousing.

The receiver was picked up again. "Nice of you to call, Cleary." Johnny's voice was beyond exasperation and approaching anger. "I've only been waiting here since two A.M. Had to call for Chinese carry-in, and let me tell you, that restaurant on the corner ain't run by no Chinese. That guy never got closer to China than Kansas."

"I thought you said Iowa."

"Iowa, Kansas, what's the difference? Neither one of them is famous for Chinese food. Now what did you need at"—there was a second's silence—"six o'clock in the morning! You better be dead or in jail,

Cleary, 'cause if you're not, you're dead and I'm in jail for killing you."

"Shut up, Betts, and listen."

"Hey, man, you sound like shit. Like maybe you swallowed sandpaper and it stuck in your throat. You been to bed yet?"

"No, I've been too busy. Now listen. A man died last night, Betts. I want you to find out everything there is to know about him."

"Is this a new case, or does it have something to do with that bail jumper? Did you have any better luck at finding him than I did?"

"Betts, the dead man is the bail jumper," explained Cleary, grinding out his cigarette with his heel.

"What would anybody want to kill him for? I mean, the bail bondsman was pretty mad, but not enough to kill him for two hundred bucks. It's not like he could collect a bounty on the guy." Johnny still sounded bleary-eyed, which was the only reason Cleary wasn't going back to the office to pull his head off and shrink it.

"Betts, you sound like you got tomato beef chow mein for brains this morning. Now shut up and let me explain." Cleary did so in as few words as he could manage, interrupted frequently with Johnny's "damn's" and "I'll be's."

There was a long silence on the other end of the line before Cleary heard Johnny clear his throat. "You know, Cleary, I can't see why we're getting involved. It's not like we've got a paying client. The bail bondsman sure isn't going to pay to find out who killed the Chinaman. It sounds like a plain vanilla murder during a robbery, and, furthermore, it sounds like a tong war. Those tongs are mean sons of bitches, and I don't think it's a good idea to stick our noses in their business. We're liable to get them chopped off."

Cleary rubbed his hand over his face. He was getting a little tired of everyone telling him to stay out of Chinatown. "This is something I have to do, Betts. It's personal. I owe somebody a debt."

"Yeah? Well, you nearly got your head blown off just yesterday paying off a personal debt. Have you forgotten Joe Quinlan?"

"No, I haven't forgotten Joe."

"You know what I think, Cleary?" asked Johnny, his voice sounding too wise for his years.

"No, but I'm sure you're going to tell me."

"Damn right I am. I think you ought to start paying cash. Every time you owe somebody, it's dangerous to your health. I think you ought to let this one go. You're in no shape to be tied up in knots again. You're frayed around the edges as it is."

Cleary thought of his hallucination. "In this case, Betts, it's dangerous to my health if I don't get involved, and you let me worry about my frayed edges."

"Talking to you is like talking to a brick wall, Cleary. You be careful, you hear?"

"Sure, kid. I'll walk like I'm skating on ice."

"Then you better wear a life preserver, because sure as shootin', you'll fall through the only hole in the pond."

FIFTEEN

Cleary parked his Eldorado in front of the old, square-brick station house on First and Hill streets. Turning off his ignition, he sat for a while, watching uniformed cops marching young thugs with greasy haircuts, old winos with stained trousers, bunko artists in loud suits, wife beaters with their knuckles still bruised, and the pros at crime, in and out of the front entrance. Everybody was protesting their innocence except the pros. They knew better. Don't talk to the cops; talk to a lawyer instead. Let him talk to the cops. It was the best way to avoid having a tired, overworked, underpaid uniform belt you across the mouth.

Cleary got out and walked into the station house.

The institutional green plaster walls were chipped, dirty, and bilious looking. The desks were old and battered, with drawer pulls missing, and legs inexpertly nailed or glued back on. The building was always cold in the winter months and too hot in the summer. It was old, rundown, with faulty plumbing and inadequate lighting. It smelled of sweat, urine, vomit, and fear. It was familiar, and it used to be home.

A young thug wearing a greasy duck's ass and three-inch burns was handcuffed to the radiator. Chewing on a matchstick and playing imaginary drums to the rock and roll beat blasting from a small radio on the desktop, the thug was swaying and oblivious, his mind, what there was of it, in some other place.

Topper Hull, a middle-aged detective sporting the world's shortest brush cut on a well-oiled skull, and wearing a starched white shirt with rolled-up sleeves and a cross-draw holster, reached over and turned off the radio.

The thug stopped his beat in midair, a sullen, surprised look on his face. "Hey, I was listening to that."

"I told you to keep that radio off, Elvis," said Hull in a resigned voice. Resigned, because the detective knew the thug didn't have sense enough to drop the subject. Resigned also because he knew he would be forced to do something about it, and he was tired of young punks. He would rather deal with a pro any day of the week. The pros knew the rules.

He stepped away from the desk toward Cleary. "It's been a while, Jack."

Cleary shook hands. Hull was a solid, unimaginative detective, but he gave it his best shot, which was more than Cleary could say for Hine and Sfakis. "I need to make a statement, Hull. Murder down in Chinatown."

"I heard about it. Gusalito'll take it," he said, pointing to a desk. "Excuse me a minute." He walked back to his own desk, where the thug had defiantly snapped the radio back on, cranked up the volume, and was returning to his imaginary skins with a vengeance.

Hull reached over, picked up the radio, and suddenly brought it down on his knee, neatly breaking it in half. He handed the two pieces back to the thug who stared dully at them. "I told you to leave the fucking thing off." He walked back to Cleary and Gusalito.

Gusalito, a younger, slimmer version of Hull, and wearing a snap-brim hat to cover his receding hairline, looked at Cleary. "We get a dozen like him every day," he said, nodding toward the thug. "Country's going to hell in a hand basket. Now let's get this statement done."

Cleary sat in the wooden chair in front of the desk and dictated his statement, hearing his voice crack and sound more hoarse as he talked. Beyond the tone of his voice, he didn't listen. He had been over the events so many times since the murder happened, he was like an automatic. He just kept firing until he was empty.

Gusalito slurped coffee out of a paper cup and laboriously typed the report as Cleary dictated. With his two index fingers, he punched the last few words. "There, that should do it, and in triplicate." He ripped the report out of the old Underwood and handed it to Cleary. "Give it a quick proofread, and we're done."

Cleary scanned it quickly, noticed the detective's

typing hadn't improved, and signed the statement. "Thanks, Gus," he said.

"Shoot-out in Chinatown. You could always draw the action, Jack. Just like a damn lightening rod. Stick you in the ground, then wait with a net to catch the falling hoods."

Hull shook his head. "You're wasting your time, Cleary. We've had a bumper crop of homicides this year. We got forty open cases just like this one, most of them in Chinatown."

Cleary glanced at the report, seeing the intellectual face of the dead Chinese instead, and put it on Gusalito's desk. "Now you got forty-one."

He got up and started toward the front entrance when he heard a boisterous commotion at the end of the hall. He turned to see Hine and Sfakis leading in a handcuffed young Chinese gang member. Sporting a duck-assed pompadour and wearing a bloodstained, yellow-and-green-satin dragon jacket, the young kid was one of a growing number of Chinese, mostly young, who straddled two cultures. They loved American rock music, haircuts, and life-style, but the dragon jackets stated emphatically that they were still Chinese, still held in thrall by the tongs.

Hine and Sfakis held out their fingers in the old V for victory sign. The other cops set up a cheer like the two had just pitched a no-hitter in the seventh game of the World Series, and the kid was the trophy. He looked like a trophy in more ways than one, thought Cleary, approaching the circle of cops surrounding the youngster. He looked like a wounded animal surrounded by joyous hunters. He also appeared to have had the shit kicked out of him recently. He glanced down at Hine's shoe and saw a red-brown smear on the toe.

"You fat slobs got me framed up," began the young Chinese, his voice almost totally void of an accent.

"I told you to shut up!" said Hine, grabbing him by the face and pinching his battered features together. "You a deaf Chinaman?"

Sfakis nudged Hine in the ribs. Hine flinched, and Cleary hoped that meant the kid had gotten back some of his own. "Look who's here," said Sfakis, his head turning on its nonexistent neck.

Cleary stopped next to the youngster and studied his eyes. The black, oblique orbs showed no sign of recognition. In fact, an expression of puzzlement mixed with hope replaced his defiant smirk, as though he saw Cleary as a chance to get out of a jam.

"I didn't do it," the kid said to Cleary with a glance back toward Hine and Sfakis. "They're framing me."

"Listen to that shit," Hine said to Sfakis.

Cleary studied the green-and-yellow-satin jacket, thumbing through his memories like index cards. "You belong to Joe Boys," he said finally.

The kid nodded, a little surprised that a Caucasian could distinguish between the various Chinese gangs. "I didn't rob nobody, mister. And I didn't kill nobody neither."

A superior sneer curled up one side of Hine's lip. "He's your killer all right, Cleary," he said in a self-satisfied voice, and Cleary realized the detective was subtly mocking him for letting a skinny kid hold him at gunpoint. "He don't scare you without this, does he?" Hine dropped the ugly sawed-off shotgun on the desk with a thud.

The Chinese boy's eyes rounded as much as his race's eyes could at the sight of the shotgun. "That's not mine! I never saw it before!"

Hine backhanded the kid across the face, cutting

off anything he wanted to say. "When I want something from you, I'll beat it out of you." Several cops snickered at the joke. Cleary felt sick.

"You're chopped suey, kid," Hine continued, dragging out his joke for the benefit of the crowd.

The kid looked at the circle of tough Caucasians surrounding him, his eyes wider than before. Turning slowly he stopped and looked defiantly into Cleary's eyes. The expressions of puzzlement and hope were gone. This foreign devil with the unshaven face was no different than the rest. He had been stupid to look at him with hope. He would not be stupid again. He flashed a message of hatred at Cleary. He was captured, but not beaten. The foreign devils could not accomplish that.

Sfakis put a mask, one of the Chinese masks used in the holdup, in front of the kid's face. For a second all Cleary could see of the boy were two blinking eyes.

"Look familiar, 'Creary'?" he asked, grinning at his Chinese pronunciation.

"You've been in Chinatown too long, Sfakis. You sound just like them. Close my eyes and I can't tell you from a tong gunman." He had the satisfaction of seeing the neckless wonder turn red.

"That's not mine!" yelled the kid, trying to push the mask away.

Sfakis punched him in the kidneys, two hard, crippling blows that sent the kid to his knees. Cleary clenched his fists to keep from delivering two punches to the same location on Sfakis's fat body. He was outnumbered, and he didn't think he would have any allies, not even Hull and Gusalito. They wouldn't understand hammering a cop over a Chink kid. And any blow the detective took from Cleary, he would double and give to the kid. That was just the way life worked. It was the order of things.

Cleary had to satisfy himself with the dirtiest look he could muster. Sfakis shrugged it off. "These gang kids are are muscling in all over Chinatown. They don't deserve any better, and it gives us credit with the tongs. They don't like them any better than we do."

Cleary watched the kid being pushed away toward the cell block. Something didn't feel right, but he couldn't pinpoint in his mind what was wrong. He needed to sort out his memories and images of last night. He looked down at the sawed-off shotgun and the Chinese clown mask on the table. Picking up the mask, he poked his finger through one of the eye-holes. He frowned again as unease prickled up his spine.

The streets of Chinatown were crowded and noisy as the people thronged in front of stores and tea-houses to shop or gossip. The scent of incense permeated the air, not so much because the Chinese couldn't live without it, as because it was a defense against clogged sewers and drains, rotting fish and vegetables, and the all-pervasive odor of too many people crowded into too small a space. Cleary had read somewhere the French perfume industry developed for much the same reasons.

A battered old half-ton truck pulled up in a cloud of diesel fumes, sloshing water all over the street. The Chinese driver jumped out, and nimbly clambered up into the back. A giant fish tank filled with equally giant catfish sat precariously in the truck bed. Gaffing a big catfish, the Chinese hurled it off the truck onto the sidewalk, where it flopped and thrashed and bled over the concrete. Cleary unconsciously stepped over it, walked next door, and stopped at the distinctive street entrance to the gambling den.

Touching the bullet holes in the door, he tried to reconstruct what had happened the night before. Maybe, just maybe, a reconstruction would pin down what was giving him an itch along his backbone. He stepped inside and walked up the same staircase he ran down last night chasing the two masked gunmen. It was the same steep staircase and orange railing, looking a little dirty and shabby in the bright morning light. Halfway up the stairs, he saw the hole blasted into the wall at head level. This was where he almost died when the masked gunman cut loose with the shotgun. Looking at the size of the hole, he wondered why he hadn't died. He must have a guardian angel, because there was no way he could've ducked that blast without help.

Guardian angel, or a ghost? He shivered as he opened the orange metal door with the symbol of the dragon swallowing its tail. Stepping inside the gambling den, he closed his eyes and recited the multiplication tables through the fives to himself. It was one way to get his mind off the supernatural and back on a rational course. Math was nothing if not rational. Two times two always equaled four. Which was more than he could say about the case. However he added or multiplied, nothing was equal.

He opened his eyes and stood still for a moment, reliving the violence that took place in this room last night. Instead of sunlight streaming through the windows, there was black, starless night. Instead of empty silence, there were voices, clicking mah-jongg tiles, the rustle of money. The hair on the back of his neck stiffened as he heard a noise where there shouldn't be one. Breathing rapidly he pulled his .38 and turned toward the windows, where the sunlight shone into his eyes, nearly blinding him. Still the rubbing sound continued, coming from the place of brightest light.

Shielding his eyes, he walked silently toward the light, his breathing quieting as he made out the figure of... He halted, stunned by the sight of a young Chinese woman, lovely in the sunlight, trying to scrub the bloodstains and chalk marks off the linoleum floor. The floor seemed to tilt, as for one terrifying moment he thought it was *her*, his ghost. But it wasn't. This woman's features were too strong, her eyes expressing too much independence.

"Who are you?" he asked hoarsely.

She looked at his gun, her features stiff with terror, and he felt like some pervert exposing himself in the public park. He looked at his gun, swallowed, and tucked it back in his holster. "Who are you?" he asked again.

"Kai-Lee, Officer," she answered, her voice having only the faintest accent.

"I'm not a cop. I'm a private investigator."

The veiled fear left her eyes, and she went back to scrubbing madly, as if her life depended on it. Who was she? he wondered. The laborer's wife? His daughter? He didn't know. "You're destroying evidence. You'll have to stop," he continued.

She kept on scrubbing the blood away, and he reached down to take her arm. "Didn't you understand me? That's evidence."

She avoided his touch, flinching away like a wounded child. Like the kid at the station house. "No. Please," she said, an imploring note in her voice that wrenched his belly. "They arrested my brother for the murder."

She bent her head, exposing the vulnerable back of her neck like a convicted woman awaiting the fall of the executioner's axe. Then she broke the spell by falling to her hands and knees and scrubbing mindlessly at the bloodstains, a pitiful, Oriental Lady Macbeth performing an act of absolution.

Cleary couldn't stand the sight of it. He reached down and gently pulled her to her feet, clasping his hands around her fragile arms. "You're destroying evidence."

She shook her head, the black cloud of silky hair flying about her head with the force of her motion. "You don't understand. He has brought enough shame on our family already with his gangs, but this . . ."

Cleary felt the anger flare, searing along his nerves. "What is it with you people? This isn't China. Shame's got nothing to do with it. Family's got nothing to do with it. It was his choice. You didn't make it, your family didn't make it. He did. He killed a guy. Wiping up the man's blood isn't going change that."

"It's not possible. He couldn't do it," she said, her eyes turning liquid with tears, and the shape of her mouth blurred by quivering.

"The shotgun and the mask they caught your brother with are the ones the holdup men used. There's no mistake. I know. I was here last night."

She grasped the lapels of his coat. A faint scent of jasmine floated like a memory through the air. "Then you know he didn't do it."

Cleary released her and stepped back, out of the range of scent-invoked memories. "Lady"—he sighed—"I don't know who did it." He realized it was the truth. He didn't believe the boy was guilty, and it wasn't just because his sister wore jasmine perfume that reminded him of someone else. It was because the boy *didn't* remind him enough of the gunman. Congratulations, Clearly, he said to himself. First you see a ghost, next you'll be reading tea leaves.

She stepped closer to him. "Help him, please. I'll give you anything you want."

The scent of jasmine was stronger, her features blurred like the image in a pool of water, and he closed his eyes. His ghost was dead. She was not this woman. Touching the warm silk that was this woman's skin would not be the same. The feel of her would not be the same. He couldn't help this woman.

"I told you," he said harshly, opening his eyes. "I'm not a cop. Why don't you go to the tong? They run things down here. Tell them to get all inscrutable, and get the kid out. But I *can't* help you."

Kai-Lee looked up at him, disillusionment in her eyes. "I should have realized. You're just like the rest of them." She gave him one last look and ran from the room, tears flowing down her golden-tinted skin.

He heard her steps clattering down the staircase and moved to the window to watch her. He frowned. The sunlight had gone, the rain streaked the window. A peal of thunder shook the building and his mind, shaking loose dust from the ceiling, and images from the closed drawers of his memory. He grabbed his head as if to keep the images locked inside, but it was too late. He remembered . . .

. . . the peal of thunder as he skidded the Narcotics Division police vehicle to a stop in front of the circle of cops and plainclothes detectives, his headlights washing over their faces. Heavy rain beat down on their hats, pouring off the brims in miniature waterfalls that threatened to deluge the cups of coffee each clutched in his hand. Steam from the coffee and smoke from their cigarettes rose to mix with the rain. He could hear the subdued laughter and isolated punch lines as they joked among themselves.

Harsh headlights from parked vehicles highlighted the ugly aftermath of a crime, illuminating the big men, throwing strange, elongated shadows over pavement and brick walls. The headlights flickered intermittently as lightning stole away their artificial illumination and encouraged the shadows to dart and spiral around in a nightmarish dance. Hine, Sfakis, a plainsclothes detective named Dibble, and a couple of uniformed cops stood drinking coffee out of paper cups, their faces alternating between brightness and shadow in time to the lightning.

Cleary jumped out of the police vehicle, leaving the door swinging behind him, not bothering with a hat or coat, and approached the circle of men. "Where is she?" he demanded.

Hine elbowed Dibble. "I told you this was bound to happen, Cleary. This is Chinatown. You stay in your place, and don't rock the boat. Not even to save your life. And that goes for cops, too."

"Shut up!" said Cleary, trying to take a breath to ease the suffocating feeling in his chest. "Just show me where she is."

Dibble spread his hands in resignation and nodded toward Hine. The other detective finished his coffee and tossed his cup in the gutter, then led Cleary down the alley. He stopped at a body covered over with a sodden, olive-colored blanket. Leaning over, he casually flipped it open with the same careless motion he used to toss away his paper cup. He stood up and watched with a half smile.

Cleary felt as if he had been hit in the belly by a sledgehammer as the lightning flashed and he saw clearly the delicate features of the Chinese prostitute. Her eyes were open, their liquid beauty dulled. Her hair lay in damp hanks about her face and shoulders, trailing down like wet seaweed against the scarlet red dress. He sank to his knees and gently touched a bronze medallion that still lay nestled between her breasts. He licked his lips and wondered at the salty taste of the rain.

The blinding light of a flashbulb went off in his face, and blinking, he looked up. The police photographer lowered his bulky camera and quickly sniffed nasal spary into his nose. "Trying to fight off a cold," he told Cleary. "Getting called out in the rain to take pictures of dead Chinese pros doesn't help any."

Cleary sat back on his heels, wondering why he couldn't find the strength to kick the photographer's nose through the back of his skull.

"You got enough?" Hine asked the photographer.

The photographer tucked his nasal spray back in his pocket and shifted the viewfinder back to his eye. "Just a couple more."

Out of the corner of his eye, Cleary saw Sfakis walk up, gaze disinterestedly at the corpse, and turn to Dibble. "I got twenty bucks says Brooklyn all the way."

Dibble snorted and wiped his nose. "Forget it, Sfakis. You still owe me for the '51 Series."

Hine shifted his feet, and Cleary no longer felt the detective's watchful gaze. "I get hungry just coming down here. Come on, Cleary, we're going to grab some chow mein."

Cleary looked up as Hine rejoined the circle of cops. A circle, never ending, with him on the outside.

He looked down at the exquisite young girl and struggled to regain his equilibrium. "I did what I could," he whispered, and knew he lied. The chilly rain saturated his shirt, and he sat unmoving, watching it pour off his unprotected head and onto the already soaked blanket.

He heard the other cops wander away to snatch meals and drinks on the cuff from Chinese owners of restaurants and bars too afraid to turn them away. He stayed, unable to stomach food. Or himself. A loud pop startled him, and he looked up into another blinding flash . . .

. . . of lightning. He looked around the empty gambling hall, and sank against the window, his hands shaking. "Oh God," he whispered, and looked out the window at the rain saturating the brilliant colors of Chinatown. He licked his lips and tasted salt.

S I X T E E N

Cleary sat at his desk in midmorning silence staring at a faded newspaper clipping, his mind running around and around like a train on a circular track, seeing the same scenery over and over again. Chinatown, the tong, the prostitute in the scarlet dress, her eyes now alive and beckoning, now dead and staring. The faded photo mocked him with his own face, pale and sick and apologetic, hair plastered against his skull by the driving rain, a glimpse of the sodden blanket and an outflung hand visible in the background. He rubbed his hand over his face, scratching his own palm against the stubble that was growing its way into a beard. He knew without looking that his blue eyes were red-rimmed and feverish looking. Another night without sleep, and he would be a candidate for the coroner. But not before he made sense of what had happened in Chinatown, both last night and five years ago. This time he wouldn't fail the victim. This time he wasn't a cop, he was a free agent. A private eye.

He reached over and picked up his cup of coffee, took a sip, frowned, and slammed his fist on the desk. "Dworski!!!"

He glared at his door until it opened, admitting Dottie, caught in midapplication of her daily makeup. He looked at her and his lips twitched. Mascara and a false eyelash adorned one eye while the other remained in pristine condition. He decided he liked it better. Two fat pink rollers peeked out of the nest of curly bangs like cherubs peeking through the clouds.

"You screamed?" she asked coolly.

"Can't you do that at home?"

"Do what?"

"Put that gunk on your face. I never know if it's Halloween, or you're going to a masquerade party."

Dottie took a deep breath and put her hands on her hips. "I'll stop using 'gunk' when you start shaving. I never know if I'm working for a private eye or an advertisement for Burma Shave."

"I've never heard any complaints before," he said.

"You ain't listened. Now what did Your Highness want?"

He held up his coffee cup. "This coffee is cold. I'd have to heat it up for icicles to form."

Dottie pranced over to the desk, glanced down at the cup, then spread her arms in mock surprise. "Well, how do you like that for thermodynamics?"

Cleary glared into her one virgin eye. "Are you taking a vocabulary course, or is that word supposed to answer my question?"

"I brought it to you over an hour ago, Cleary. You're supposed to drink it while it's hot."

He glanced at his watch, then buried his head in his hands, feeling totally disoriented. An hour? Jesus, he had to work. He couldn't sit around reliving the past, or the past was going to repeat itself. He heard Dottie step around the desk to stand by his shoulder. He raised his head. "Sorry, Dottie."

She patted him, glancing over his shoulder at the desk. "Everybody's got a right to be cranky once in a while." Her voice faded as her curiosity got the best of her and she focused on the faded newspaper clipping extracted from a nearby folder crammed with police-related memorabilia.

He covered up his photograph taken at the crime scene, but the headline, CHINATOWN PROSTITUTE FOUND MURDERED, stared up at him from the inconspicuous page ten article. He shoved the clipping back in the folder. "Heard from Betts?" he asked calmly.

Dottie stepped back as Cleary stood and grabbed his coat. "Yeah, he called. I told him you didn't want to be disturbed. That's when I thought you were catching a nap." Her eyes told him he would have been better off doing that than looking at old photos as she handed him a note. "He said he's got the info you wanted."

Cleary shrugged into his coat as he rounded his desk. "Tell him to sit tight." He straightened his collar, his mind dancing backward. "I've got a stop to make first."

He started through the door, then stopped and turned to smile at Dottie. "Friends again?"

Dottie smiled. "Sure, Cleary. Just try to get some sleep, huh?"

"Sure. When I have time," he said, taking a step through the door.

"Cleary?"

He stopped, and looked over his shoulder. "Yeah, what do you need?"

"Watch yourself in Chinatown. I heard it's bad news down there."

"You're nagging, Dottie," he said, getting all the way through the door this time.

"Cleary?"

He stopped again, but didn't bother to look at her.

"Get a shave."

He didn't answer and made it all the way down stairs and out the door.

A pair of ancient hands, working with infinite care, slowly placed a ginseng root into the nearly finished swirl pattern in a black lacquer box. Her hands were gnarled, much like the small roots of the ginseng she touched. Her placement was perfect. The swirl was exquisite in its beauty, an art form of another world.

Along the long counter, other hands transformed the ginseng roots into intricate mosaics to adorn other boxes. Each box was at a different stage of design, beginning with a sunburst in the very center, then working outward, each individual root fitting into a space that only it could occupy—like a Chinese puzzle.

It was the artistic expression of the order of things, thought Cleary, standing in the aisle of the Chinese herb shop and watching the ginseng ritual taking place in front of him. There was a timeless elegance to the Chinese women's motion. But it was a com-

ment on their world and their sense of order that all
the ginseng patterns were alike. There was no place
for the individual who might want to alter that pattern. Such a woman would simply be cast out and
another take her place, like the dead whose name and
place was passed along to another.

He shuddered, feeling very foreign all of a sudden
in this environment, surrounded by all manner of
strange and exotic Far Eastern herbs, spices, omen
powders, and Chinese remedies from rhino-horn
powder and dried snakeskins to shark fins. He was in
the midst of a far-flung outpost of an ancient civiliza-
tion, and he was about to challenge the very root of
the order of things.

The women fell silent, looking at someone behind
Cleary for downcast eyes. He turned around and saw
Ko-Chen Lu, a young, thin Chinese man who motioned him to follow. With a last glance at the old
women, he trailed after Ko-Chen Lu to the rear of the
store and into a step-up back office resting on a raised
platform.

Tendrils of the inevitable incense smoke floated
past photographs commemorating past presidents of
the tong, a bronze statue of Tien Hau, Queen of
Heaven, sitting next to a portrait of Eisenhower, au-
tographed to Uncle Lu. It was a typical Chinatown
arrangement, thought Cleary. The power of the Caucasian world was acknowledged, but given no more
emphasis than long-dead leaders of a strictly illegal
Chinese quasi—criminal organization.

Four Chinese elders sat around a table cluttered by
invoices and sales slips. Smoldering joss sticks
burned around the room, filling it with a cloying
sweetness. An old Chinese man sat in the corner
working on an abacus at incredible speed, faster than

a banker could operate an adding machine. The sound of the rhythmical clicking, along with the incense-saturated air, was hypnotic. Cleary found himself trying to blink away the effects.

Some of the men sipped tea. Others nibbled on fruit while they sat quietly waiting. They didn't look like much, thought Cleary: simple clothes, polite manners, bland, kindly faces. To anyone unfamiliar with Chinatown, they looked like small shop owners. Which only proved how dangerous Chinatown could be for the unwary, because these insignificant-looking old men, greeting him respectfully with almost imperceptible smiles and nods, were the powerful tong overlords. They controlled the order of things by threat of death.

Ko-Chen Lu took a seat next to a frail old man whose skin looked translucent, like very thin sheets of ancient yellowed ivory coating his bones. The old man seemed only vaguely aware of what was going on in the room, a gentle great-grandfather on the verge of senility. Another misleading impression. Cleary knew that frail old man was the single most powerful individual in Chinatown.

Cleary bowed slightly to the old man, who made only the slightest of motions back, and not because of age. Uncle Lu was aware of his status and bowed deeply to no one, if he bowed at all. "*Ni how ma*, Uncle Lu," he said, and waited until Ko-Chen Lu, looking almost robust compared to the old one, whispered something into Uncle Lu's ear.

"*Ni how ma*, Cleary," said Uncle Lu in a voice both hollow sounding and quivering as he nodded greetings. "Would you like tea?" he asked, using Ko-Chen Lu as his interpreter.

Cleary nodded and sat down in obedience to Uncle

Lu's unspoken invitation. He waited silently while the old man poured steaming tea into a bone cup and slid it in front of him.

"You are well?" asked Uncle Lu, again through Ko-Chen Lu, and Cleary wondered why the old man bothered with the pretense that he needed an interpreter, except that it was a good ploy when Uncle Lu didn't want to talk to Caucasians. Which happened to be most of the time. Still, it made for a stilted conversation.

"I am well, Uncle Lu," he finally answered, studying the old man and learning, as usual, nothing except what Uncle Lu wanted him to find.

"You have sons yet?"

Cleary felt his face redden. "No. My wife and I are no longer married."

The old man nodded in disapproval. "It is not good. A man must have a wife and sons. Who else will see to his burial?" To Uncle Lu and to most Chinese of his age and younger, an unmarried man was suspect, a deviation from the order of things.

Cleary shrugged. "It didn't work out." An image of a delicate girl in a scarlet dress flashed in his mind, and he frowned.

"She was not for you," said Uncle Lu.

Cleary didn't bother wondering how the old man could read his thoughts. "I didn't have much time to find out for myself, did I?" he asked, and knew the bitterness in his voice was out of place in this room.

"She was not for you," repeated Uncle Lu. "Drink your tea."

Cleary picked up the cup, his hatred for this old man and all he stood for making his hands tremble. He took a sip, held it in his mouth, then swallowed. He repeated the ritual several times, until his rage subsided. He just wished to hell the old man would talk to him directly. "It is good," he finally said.

"We heard about the unfortunate incident at the tables last night," said Uncle Lu, as if no other topic of conversation had been discussed.

Cleary laughed humorlessly. "Unfortunate is right."

Uncle Lu shook his head sorrowfully. "Thankfully the police have captured the boy who did it. The youth of today do not show proper respect."

"I hardly think respect is the right word to use about murder. If the kid did do it." He let his voice die and studied the faces around the table. As usual, he could read nothing from their faces. They simply stared back at him as if he were a specimen under a microscope. "I find it peculiar that the cops were able to find this Chinese kid before you did."

Uncle Lu raised his bony hand in a deprecating gesture and laughed. "I think you always overestimated our little merchants' association. We hear things—rumors, gossip—but we do not know everything that goes on in Chinatown."

"A merchants' association?" asked Cleary with a laugh. "That's a new public relations move. But call your group whatever you like, it still controls Chinatown. When I was in Vice down here, and a Chinaman committed a crime, we didn't find out about it until his body washed up in Long Beach. Your 'association' was pretty effective at crime control."

The only response he got was the sipping of tea and the reflection of overhead lights off three pairs of steel-rimmed glasses. He always wondered if these old men deliberately sat where the light would blank out their eyes if the need arose.

Looking back to Uncle Lu, he spoke directly,

knowing Ko-Chen Lu wouldn't want to translate ac-
curately and knowing it didn't matter because Uncle
Lu spoke perfect English anyway. "I remember a time
when the tong would never have allowed something
so bad for business."

Ko-Chen Lu finally spoke for himself. "We are finally becoming assimilated."

Uncle Lu nudged him to interpret. "Let the police-
men keep the streets safe," said the old man. "It is
their place." He gave Cleary a small smile. "Is that not
what you always wanted us to do? Now we are doing
it."

"We are confident that this will be the end of these
robberies..." said Ko-Chen Lu in another speech for
himself. However, he didn't finish because Uncle Lu
cut him off with a look that should have sent the
younger man to join his ancestors.

But Ko-Chen Lu had said enough as far as Cleary
was concerned. "Robberies? You mean to tell me this
isn't the first? Somebody's running around knocking
off your gambling dens?" He shook his head in an
imitation of shocked surprise. "You guys are starting
to lose your touch."

He continued shaking his head, a man deeply per-
turbed, disappointed, perhaps even frightened by this
evidence of a crack in the order of things. The old
men did not move or frown, but there was a tightening of hands about tea cups, a hesitation as fingers
selected another piece of fruit, a faint tremor in the
rigid posture. Cleary felt smug. For the first time
since he had met these tong leaders many years ago,
he had managed to make them uncomfortable.

"If these gang kids get any more confident, this
place is going to be up for grabs. Then you'll have to
bow respectfully to them, kids young enough to be

your grandchildren, kids who'll laugh at old men like you and your talk of the order of things."

Uncle Lu smiled as Cleary's response was translated, a smile that was just a little too wide. Like a man trying to sell a house with a leaky roof. "I'm sure our troubles are over, Cleary. Now if you will excuse us." He stood up, and the rest of the Chinese men stood up with him. A polite dismissal if the private eye had ever seen one. Of course, the Chinese were always polite—even while they were killing you.

Cleary rose and bowed again to Uncle Lu, then to each of the others. "It has been a pleasure." Private eyes could be polite, too, and mean it just as little.

He stepped down from the office and stopped to light a cigarette and watch the old women perform their ginseng root ritual again. He touched one of the boxes and pantomimed his pleasure. The toothless crone decorating it covered her mouth and smiled. He felt like a hypocrite. The ginseng boxes were beautiful, yes, but he had seen a thousand just like them. He actually was interested in listening to the old men's conversation after he left.

He didn't have long to wait.

"Keep him close. Cleary may be useful to us in this matter." Cleary smiled to himself. His struggle to learn Chinese had been worth it after all. Now all he had to do was figure what 'matter' Uncle Lu was talking about.

S E V E N T E E N

It was the hull of a ship of hell, thought Cleary as he and Johnny walked down a narrow flophouse hallway. His senses were assaulted from all directions: cooking smells, water running, toilets flushing, babies crying, voices shrill with anger or soft with despair. He heard more despair than anger. These people were beyond anger; it took too much energy for anger, and none of the denizens had any to spare. They used all their energy just surviving. Besides, it was not Chinese to rage against fate.

"Jesus," said Johnny. "How do they stand it?"

"No choice," replied Cleary. "They each have their place."

"Forget that idea," said the younger man. "If I was one of them, I'd look for a better place."

"Not if you were Chinese," said Cleary, too tired to try to explain.

The dim light bulbs illuminated men coming home from hard labor, and other men just leaving, coming out of doorways, towels thrown over their shoulders, on the way to the communal toilets. They all stopped, the weary and the not so weary, pressed themselves against the walls, and watched Cleary and Johnny move past, as if they had never seen white strangers in their place before. And they probably hadn't, thought Cleary. A Chinese flophouse wasn't on the regular Chinatown tour.

"Jesus," muttered Johnny again, hunching his shoulders together under the black leather jacket, plainly uncomfortable at being somewhere he didn't belong. He stared almost rudely as they passed by rooms housing families of ten eating together in an eight-by-ten space. And not only eating, but sleeping, dressing, making love, and dying, all in that same small room. Cleary noticed him turning his head when they passed by other rooms housing men coughing their lungs out with TB.

Johnny stuck his hands in his pockets and resolutely looked straight ahead. Cleary observed that he was pale and sweating a little. "Never saw anything like it, Cleary."

Cleary nodded. "It's not what we're used to, even in the L.A. slums."

"Nah, I'm talking about the place where the guy worked, the soap factory."

"He's got a name. His name is Tao," said Cleary.

Johnny nodded, his eyes widening a little at the

sharp tone in Cleary's voice. "Yeah, right. You could pass right by the building and never know what's going on underground. All these Chinese guys in the dark, I mean. Working on top of each other. I don't know, man. I come from the hills of Appalachia and I've never seen anything like this. Vats with this stuff bubbling up like some witch is cooking brew for Halloween. It burns your eyes worse than tear gas. It was hell, man. They oughta form a union, call a strike. I mean, man, nobody ought to have to work in a place like that. It's un-American."

"This is Chinatown, Johnny."

"This is hell, you mean."

"If they had a choice," Cleary said, gesturing at the silent men still watching them, "they'd pick hell. But they don't have a choice."

Johnny looked at him as if he were speaking some incomprehensible language, and Cleary guessed he was. At least to someone who didn't know China-town.

Johnny stopped at a doorway. "This is where he lived," he said, as if he didn't really understand why anyone would live there.

Cleary stepped inside. Beds jammed the room from wall to wall, filled with men sleeping or just lying there, their eyes vacant as they thought of a home-land halfway around the world.

"That's his 'place' over there," said Johnny, point-ing to an empty bed in the corner.

Cleary edged through the room toward Tao's bed. It was different from the others, extremely neat, with a low, small bookshelf and meager belongings lying around waiting for their owner to return. A small Buddhist shrine with a photo of a younger Tao and a pretty wife and small daughter occupied one end of the bookshelf. Cleary examined the books, mostly in English, and entirely on advanced engineering. He picked up one book written in Chinese.

"Tao wrote that book," said a man's faintly accented voice.

Cleary and Johnny turned to see Frank Tang standing in the doorway, looking as trim and pleasant as always. The Chinese bar owner stepped into the room. "He was a respected man in China. He built bridges."

Cleary rubbed his hands over the book absently as he looked at Tang. "How did you know we were here?"

Tang shrugged his shoulders in an exaggerated gesture. "Everyone in Chinatown knows you are asking about this man. I knew you would come here—some time."

Johnny took the book out of Cleary's hands and looked at it as if it were magic. Cleary thought that to Johnny it probably was, engineering being as far over his head as it was to most of the others in this flophouse.

"Why would a guy smart enough to write this jump bail on a nickel-and-dime grocery store stick-up?" Johnny asked.

Tang smiled pleasantly, except Cleary noticed the pleasantness didn't reach his eyes. "Tao didn't make enough money to bring his family over. He couldn't wait any longer." His voice dropped. "He didn't have the necessary patience."

"To hell with patience," snapped Cleary, rage at the waste tightening his belly. "He was a professional man. He wrote books. What was he doing in a soap factory?"

Tang shrugged, looking at the empty bed. "He was an engineer—who made soap."

A young Chinese man came into the room, hesitated for a moment when he saw Caucasian faces, then sat down on Tao's bed. He took Tao's photo down and replaced it with one of himself taken with a pretty young wife and two older parents.

"Hey, man," said Johnny. "The other guy hasn't even been buried yet."

"His place is needed," said Tang, his pleasant smile gone.

"And his name?" asked Cleary. "Or can he at least keep that?"

Tang stiffened imperceptibly. "It is not good to speak of such things."

Cleary watched the young Chinese man leaf through Tao's books, then stack them together in a pile on the floor, like so much trash to be disposed of. "Let's get out of here, Johnny," he said, and walked mindlessly from the room. It wasn't until he climbed in the Eldorado that he realized his hands were balled into fists.

The neon lights looked subdued in the dusk, like fireflies that only danced unnoticed until darkness. Cleary felt disoriented again. Where had the day gone since he and Johnny left the flophouse? Had he been driving aimlessly through Chinatown, lecturing Johnny on Chinese customs, from midmorning until dusk? Judging from the look of stupefied boredom on Johnny's face, the answer was yes.

"Sorry," he muttered. "School's out."

Johnny blinked. "Huh? Oh, yeah. Well, I haven't been listening much. I mean, it's interesting and all, but I wouldn't be caught dead living down here."

"That's right. You'd be caught dead because you don't know enough about Chinatown to stay alive," he said as he slammed the chrome lady on the Eldorado's hood to a stop only a millimeter from the candy-flaked back end of a '54 De Soto.

Johnny cracked his knuckles as the disbelieving faces of two Chinese gang members appeared out of both the De Soto's windows. "I'm not so sure, Cleary. Things are changing."

"Not in Chinatown," said Cleary, as the two gang members, wearing greased pompadours and yellow-and-black-satin dragon jackets, got out and elaborately checked to see if there was even the slightest contact between the vehicles.

Johnny flipped up the collar of his leather jacket as he stared past the gleaming chrome hood ornament at the two Chinese kids. "I'd say especially in Chinatown."

Cleary shook his head at the stupidity of the young and slid out of the car. "Come on. It's right up the street."

There was no answer, and he turned around to see a shoot-out, street-gang style. Johnny was locked into a killer-street stare down with the gang members. He slipped out of the Caddy with the loose-limbed deliberation of a gunfighter out to make his reputation.

"I'll stay with the car," he said, not taking his eyes off the gang members. He gracefully slid onto the hood, and struck a pose of such total insouciance, so cool, so right, that Cleary saw the gang members begin to doubt themselves in their own neighborhood. Johnny broke a walnut with a loud crunching and popped the contents into his mouth. The two Chinese kids surrendered and broke eye contact.

Everybody knew a guy couldn't stare down a dragon so this Caucasian must be a dragon in disguise.

Cleary shook his head in amazement and walked on down the street. Leave it to Betts to know his place better than the Chinese kids. After all, Betts probably came from a long line of streetfighters, and tradition counted for a lot in Chinatown.

He checked out a small, simple sign on the glass window of a run-down storefront—MODERN DANCE STUDIO—and entered the building. He could hear the modern jazz playing on an inexpensive phonograph before he opened the door. The music was tinny sounding because of the cheap equipment, but to the line of ten-year-old Chinese girls, it was the beautiful sound of a world beyond Chinatown. He stopped in the doorway, watching the heartbreakingly beautiful, sweet-faced, wide-eyed little girls as they desperately tried to get the steps right to a dance as alien to them as his own blue eyes. Some watched themselves in the mirrored walls, intent on mastering this strange expression of art.

Kai-Lee glided in front of the line of little girls, and Cleary's breath caught in his throat. Wearing a dance leotard that molded itself against the lines of a body that was an artistic expression of its own, the fragile Chinese woman looked exquisite against the backdrop of the stark room. She demonstrated the dance step with a fluid style and grace in vivid contrast to the floor-scrubbing, pleading woman in the gambling den.

Cleary walked further into the studio and saw the students' mothers seated quietly on a bench. They watched, timeless, puzzled relics from another century, as their daughters danced to a sound of a time and a place they would never understand.

Kai-Lee walked gracefully over to reset the record, when a Chinese laborer pushed past Cleary into the room. He let loose a barrage of angry Chinese at one of the cringing mothers, and then grabbed a tiny frightened dancer by the hand and began dragging her to the door.

Kai-Lee dropped the needle on the phonograph, and it dug a groove across the plastic with a spine-shivering screech. Not even hearing the sound, she rushed to intercept the father, placing her body between him and the door.

"Mr. Hua, please," she begged, and Cleary heard an echo of this morning's pleading woman.

"No dance! No dance!" stated the laborer furiously.

"Please," she asked again, but her voice was resigned.

The laborer waved her away with disdain. "Foolish woman! No dance!"

He pulled the tearful little girl out the door, with the shamed mother hurrying after them. Another mother, recognizing her place in the order of things and ashamed of challenging it, got up and, taking her little girl, waddled out the door.

Kai-Lee, her shoulders slumping in dejection, lifted her hand to stop them, then let it fall. Her eyes watched the door with a kind of resignation, then refocused on Cleary, widening as she recognized him. Hesitating only a moment to weigh what his presence might mean, she turned back to the girls and clapped her hands.

"Class dismissed," she said, her voice light and pleasant again as she practiced her skills at being polite in the face of humiliation.

Actually, thought Cleary as he followed Kai-Lee into her office, Chinese women had raised being po-

lite in the face of humiliation to an art form. Practic
makes perfect, and no one had more practice at tha
particular art form than a Chinese woman. Sellin
one's daughter into prostitution, abandoning an in
fant girl to die, binding a baby's feet to grow into hid
eous, misshapen lumps of flesh, were all custom
that had lingered into the twentieth century. Some
times Cleary wondered why the women didn'
slaughter every male over the age of ten.

Cleary examined the tiny room that was Kai-Lee'
office and found it as unpretentious as the woma
who decorated it. Photos of popular modern dancers
and smaller pictures of her students lined the walls
He took one of the class photos off the wall and stud
ied it.

Kai-Lee cleared her throat. "They think it's frivo
lous." She waved her hand in a graceful dancer's ges
ture. "They would rather see their daughters learnin
to sew or work a cash register."

She stood uneasily for a moment, then turned to
small stove and lit a flame underneath an ultramod
ern, art deco whistling teakettle. Finally she turne
back to face him. "They don't understand that thi
training could help their daughters go into th
world."

Cleary hung the picture back on the wall. "The
don't want their daughters to go into the world. The
might learn something frivolous, like the fact tha
their names belong to themselves."

Kai-Lee avoided looking at him, but he saw th
same knowledge in the eyes so steadfastly starin
over his shoulder at the studio. "I looked into you
brother's case," he continued, changing the subject t
the one both of them had been avoiding. "What he
needs is a good lawyer."

Kai-Lee looked up at him, hope still lingering deep in her eyes. Like Fontana's, he thought suddenly. 'Tommy's been in trouble all his life. But I know in my heart my brother could not have done something like this. I raised him since he was five years old."

He studied her face for a long moment and saw in her eyes the unalterable truth of what she believed. He frowned, remembering his own sense of unease. "Kids can go off the track."

She ignored him, and taking a key chain from around her neck, unlocked her desk drawer. She carefully, almost reverently, as if she were handling a treasure beyond price, took out a shoebox and set it on the desk in front of Cleary.

"I found out what a private investigator does. He helps people for money."

"I'm sorry, there's nothing I can do for you." He pushed the words past a painful obstruction in his throat.

She opened the shoebox and dumped the entire contents on the table in front of Cleary. A small stack of old bills amounting to perhaps two hundred dollars, ancient jewelry, gold, and a few jade trinkets tumbled out. A gold ring rolled across the desk, and he stared, mesmerized, as she caught it in her slim ivory-skinned hand. She clutched it for a moment, then gently laid the ring on top of the pile of money and desperately pushed the whole collection toward him.

"It's everything I have," she said, looking at him while a blush of embarrassment reddened her cheeks.

The teakettle whistled, and she bit her lip and turned toward the sound. Cleary didn't move as he stared down at all the valuables a single woman

owned. The shrill whistle continued, rising and fall
ing in intensity like the...

... sound of a siren ripping through the night, out
side on the streets of Chinatown. He felt again the
heat, the stifling closeness of the room that the ceil
ing fan, turning lazily above the bed, did nothing to
alleviate. The sheets were coarsely woven cotton, and
scratched his nude body unpleasantly. The neon light
outside the window flashed vivid red and yellow
colors over his bare chest. Leaning across the rum
pled sheets, he ground out his cigarette in the cheap
glass ashtray. Resting on his elbow, he watched
smoke spiral up from a still-burning, lipstick-stained
cigarette abandoned in the ashtray. She did that a lot,
lit cigarettes and forgot them, Cleary thought.

She walked out of the shadows, pulling her scarlet
dress over her head. He hated that dress. It reminded
him of what she was, and what he didn't want her to
be. "Don't go," he said, reaching to rub his hand up
the nylon-clad thigh exposed by the slit in the Chi
nese dress. "I want you," he added huskily, trying to
entice her away from her other life and into his, be
cause she satisfied more than his lust.

She stood still, pressing his hand tightly against
her flesh, expressions of desire and resignation fight
ing for supremacy in her eyes. "I've already gotten
you in trouble with your bosses."

"That'll blow over," he said, his hand finding the
warm silky flesh above her garter. "And if it doesn't,
to hell with them."

Giving him a disbelieving smile, she turned her
back and lifted the black skein of hair out of his way.
He sighed and zipped up her dress. Her charm, a
small, simple bronze medal, had slipped around her
neck and now hung down her back. He sat up and

lipped it back around to lay between her breasts. He gently cupped her, pressing the pert nipple against his palm, before he reluctantly released her.

"I talked to the tong myself. They have no problem with you," he continued as she picked up her cigarette. She glanced over her shoulder at him, and he attempted to explain. "Everyone seems happy with the arrangement."

He reached for her again, and she avoided his hand, looking at him with her oblique, fathomless eyes. "There's nothing more I can do for you. My hands are tied."

The image of the hopeless and resigned look in her eyes lingered with him long after she left, the bronze charm glittering defiantly around her neck...

... as another siren blasted through the streets below Kai-Lee's studio. Cleary's vision cleared, and he stared down at the dance teacher's life savings as she returned with two bowls of tea and carefully set them on the wooden desk.

He reached out, proud that his hand wasn't shaking as hard as his heart was pounding, and picked up a small bronze charm, very common and very inexpensive. "I'll take this."

She looked at him like a startled doe. "But it's worth nothing."

He closed his fingers around it, and for an infinitesimal beat of time, felt the warmth of human flesh. "It'll be plenty."

EIGHTEEN

Cleary followed the jailer along the row of cells. Some things never changed, he thought, recognizing a few denizens. He had arrested these same guys, for these same crimes, when he was working for the department. They were black, white, Mexican; color didn't matter. They were rich, poor, desperate; money didn't matter. They were abused children, privileged children, benignly neglected children; parents didn't matter. They were illiterate, functional, intellectual; education didn't matter. They were loved, hated, tolerated; emotional attachments didn't matter. They all shared one common denominator: like Frank Tucci, they wanted more. Whether money, sex, or power, they wanted more. In spite of what the sociologists with all the initials after their names were saying these days, the basis of all crime was the same: more.

He didn't think that could be said of the Chinese kid whose cell the jailer was unlocking. "You got ten minutes, Cleary. Yell if he gets smart, but I don't think he will. We pretty much kicked the shit out of him."

"I noticed," said Cleary, looking at the bruised, exhausted boy lying on the bunk.

The kid roused enough to look at Cleary, then turned his attention back to the ceiling, ignoring the private eye.

"Your sister sent me," said Cleary, holding up the charm he took from Kai-Lee. The kid glanced at it, then looked at the ceiling again.

Cleary felt tempted to shake the kid, or ask him what in the hell was so interesting about that ceiling. "She thinks you got a bum rap. She's hired me to prove it."

"Tell her to save her money," the kid answered, without losing interest in the ceiling.

"What's your name, kid?" asked Cleary, stowing the charm in his pocket and lighting a cigarette.

"Tommy."

"What's your real name?"

That got his attention. He turned his head to look at Cleary. "You couldn't pronounce it," his voice revealing his surprise that a Caucasian would even know he had another name.

"Try me," said Cleary, smiling a challenge.

"San-Tsiang Tsien," said the kid smugly.

"San-Tsiang Tsien," said Cleary, pronouncing it perfectly.

The kid sat up in the bunk and grinned in spite of himself. "Not bad."

"For a foreign devil," offered Cleary.

San-Tsiang grinned again. "Yeah, I guess so."

Cleary leaned against the wall. "Give me something to work with. Help me prove you didn't do it."

"I *did* do it," said San-Tsiang.

Cleary was stunned. "What are you talking about?"

San-Tsiang shrugged. "I lied before. But it was me all right."

Cleary took a drag off his cigarette and considered the kid, his feeling of unease growing. "You weren't the guy with the shotgun. I looked in his eyes. You must've been the other guy."

The Chinese boy nodded. "You got it."

"The one with the Army-issue .45."

"Yeah, that's right."

Cleary flicked some ash into the corner, and took another drag. "That's funny. The other guy had a two-inch .38."

San-Tsiang paled under his bruises and lay down on his bunk again, facing the ceiling.

"Your jailer tells me you had visitors this morning. The merchants' association. They told you to take the fall."

"Five years, ten years in the joint"—the boy shrugged—"there's worse things that could happen to a guy."

Cleary stared at the boy, then deliberately snuffed out his cigarette in disgust and yanked him off the bunk. Dragging him to the cell door, he stuck his head against the bars. "You see those guys in the other cells? You think they're decent citizens waiting to lend a hand to a Chink kid trying to learn the ropes in the joint? They're gonna kick the shit out of you every time you stick your nose out of your cell. And that's the best thing they might do to you. You'll come out of your five or ten years in a lot worse shape than when you went in. If you come out at all."

He turned the boy around and looked directly into his eyes. "Now suppose you tell me again about how you murdered Tao?"

San-Tsiang's eyes were set and staring. And filled with infinite fatalism. "I did it," he repeated doggedly.

Cleary pushed him gently back on the bunk. "That won't work with me, kid. I'm not letting them throw away a life this time."

Cleary tucked in his shirt, stretched his arms out their full length, flexed his fingers like a musician readying himself for a concert, then picked up a stainless-steel Halliburton briefcase and placed it on his desk. Popping the lock, he opened it and extracted from the custom-molded interior an assortment of state-of-the-art electronic eavesdropping equipment: miniature bugs as small as his fingernail, transmitters and transistors looking like something out of a futuristic science-fiction movie. Cleary could almost imagine little green men from Mars every time he ordered new equipment.

"Good luck if you're planning on bugging the tong, Cleary. You're gonna need it," Johnny said, picking up a transistor and gazing at it as if it were magic. "I mean, securitywise, those cats make the mob look like a Knights of Columbus open house. Besides, your eyes are the wrong color, and they squint the wrong way. So what are you planning? You got some ace up your boxers or what?"

Cleary smacked Johnny's paw away from a particularly delicate device, then returned to checking out his equipment. "Let's just say I've worked those streets before."

Johnny gave a jerk of a nod. "Okay, Cleary. Don't tell me. I mean I'm not going to lose any sleep, but unless you need a chaperone, I was thinking about trackin' down the Joe Boys. Feel them out on what they know about their boy in the slammer."

Cleary looked up, surprised out of his preoccupation. "I appreciate your initiative, Betts, but what makes you think they'll even give you the time of day? Those kids fell between the cracks the day they were born. They're so disenfranchised, they're practically alien life-forms."

Johnny pulled a comb out of his pocket and ran it through his pompadour. "I ain't exactly a Norman Rockwell poster, boss."

Cleary looked at him: thirty-weight, gravity-defying hair, black boots, black leather jacket worn in ninety-degree weather, speech consisting of English words found in any dictionary, with meanings found in no dictionary. Betts had a point. Set a thief to catch a thief; set an alien to catch an alien. Actually Betts qualified as both, but in a good cause, he reminded himself.

The intercom buzzed, and Cleary hit the button while still studying his streetwise employee. "Yeah?"

"There's someone here to see you," said Dottie in between popping her gum.

"Not now, Dottie," he said, snapping off the intercom, and handing Johnny a slip of paper. "The stakeout'll be set up in room 220, the hotel across the street from the herb shop."

"That fleabag?"

"Not many four-star hotels in Chinatown," replied Cleary, thinking that that fleabag actually complimented his quarters. He would be lucky if fleas were all that shared space with him.

Johnny nodded and turned to leave. "See you later, alligator."

"Betts?"

"Yeah?" said Johnny, turning back around.

"Be careful. These Chinese gangs don't take prisoners."

Johnny opened his mouth to reply, when Dottie opened the door, a pencil stuck through the mass of curls anchored at the crown of her head.

"Dottie, I told you—"

"You'll want to see this someone," she said, overriding his objection.

Cleary debated spelling out the words, "not now," but judging from the letters Dottie typed for him, spelling and Dottie had only a nodding acquaintance.

Before he had a chance to formulate some subtle way of convincing Dottie that when he said no he meant no, Kai-Lee stepped through the doorway. He lost track of what he was trying to say, lost track, too, of what he had been about to do, or had been doing, for that matter. Kai-Lee looked completely exotic in the narrow definition of the word: completely out of place, foreign, and completely outside time, timeless. Faintly he heard Dottie and Betts shuffle out the door and close it. He was alone with her.

Rounding the desk, he approached her with the same care he would use approaching any rare and beautiful object. But Kai-Lee was not an object: she was real and warm and intensely feminine. And he wanted to touch her.

She stepped away just as he raised his hand, a determined look in her eyes. "I want you to stop."

He was disoriented again, lost on a personal, sensual plane of thought, and she was obviously speaking professionally, as his client. He had been disoriented so much during this case, he wondered if he might be developing a split personality.

He cleared his throat, the tone of her voice finally sinking in. "You came prepared with that little speech, didn't you? It sounded memorized. Now suppose you tell me what caused this change of heart. What's happened, Kai-Lee?"

Her lashes fluttered, but Cleary knew it had nothing to do with flirtation. Long lashes were useful for veiling eyes when you didn't want anyone guessing your thoughts.

"I made a mistake. Tommy says that he is guilty. I'm sorry."

"What does San-Tsiang Tsien say? Does he say he's guilty, too?"

Her lashes whipped apart and she looked at him. Cleary knew he had scored a body blow, because her eyes had a stunned look. "I can't walk away from this, Kai-Lee. Nobody's gonna take your brother's name."

She backed away from him, her arms crossed in front of her face, palms outward, like a woman warding off an assailant. "Don't come back to Chinatown, Cleary. Please. Just leave us alone."

Cleary watched another night descend on Chinatown, sparkling with neon, scented with incense, and melodious with the singsong sounds of Chinese voices. Her citizens came out to greet her: the gamblers, the pimps, the prostitutes, ready to begin their night's work; the weary laborers, freed from theirs and wending their way back to the flophouses; the homeless, searching for discarded food in the gutters and alleys. It never changed, this endless cycle of Chinatown.

He shifted his feet, leaned more heavily against the

Eldorado, and watched Charlie Fontana work on a dim sum order from a nearby vendor. "He was winning, Charlie. This guy was just standing there, and for the first time in his life he was winning. He had a chance to make things different."

Cleary stopped to light a cigarette and looked out over the streets until he regained control of his voice. "Now he's pushing up grass. You tell me that's the way it was supposed to be."

Fontana chewed silently, his face scrunched up in lines. He swallowed and looked at Cleary. "Trying to make sense of things that happen in this part of town's a good way to drive a person crazy, Jack."

Cleary inhaled deeply, the acrid smoke matching his mood. "His last few hours in America and he was gambling like a madman, trying to make money for his family back in China. That's why he robbed the grocery store. He wanted to bring his wife and daughter over."

"A tough break," said Fontana in a tone of voice that said cops saw lots of tough breaks. "But we *got* the guy that did it."

Cleary flipped his cigarette in the gutter. "I'll believe that when the Easter bunny leaves me a chocolate egg."

"Come on, Jack. The kid says he did it, the sister says he did it, and the tong says he did it. What do you want? An affidavit from God?"

"Yeah, maybe I do, Charlie. Because I think everybody's lying. The kid and his sister because they're afraid of the tong, but why is the tong lying? Who the hell are they afraid of? These gangs of kids? I don't think so. The tong is selling San-Tsiang Tsien down the river because it's one way to restore order in Chinatown. Well, to hell with the tong."

Fontana grabbed his arm. "You're reading more into this than there is. You're fighting old battles."

Cleary slid off the car. "I'm not fighting old battles. I never fought the last time." He opened the Caddy's door and slipped in. "It was good to see you, Charlie."

Fontana leaned in the open window. "You can't change something that happened five years ago. This Chinatown arrangement goes back aways, Jack."

"You mean the arrangement between the cops and the tong?" interrupted Cleary, feeling rage tighten his muscles.

Fontana's face went rigid. "It's not exactly what you think, Jack. It never was. Sure, sometimes we close an eye to the tong's gambling dens and some of their other activities because they're the only law in Chinatown. The cops are here on sufferance, and because the tong finds it easier to accommodate us than fight us. Sure, we could take over from them, but we'd have to wade knee-deep in blood and bodies to do it. Without the tong, this whole section will explode. But we don't let them get away with murder."

"Don't you?" asked Cleary, catching the faintest scent of jasmine on the evening air.

"Damn it, Jack, if you ever accuse me of anything like that again, I'll knock your stubborn head right off your shoulders." Fontana expelled a deep breath. "We don't know who killed that girl five years ago. While you were eating guilt for breakfast, lunch, and dinner, I looked into it. There was nothing. If I had found some smell that it was a tong killing, I would've done something. What, I don't know. You know how it is."

"Yeah. That's why I transferred out of Chinatown. I couldn't stand facing it every day."

"Facing the tong, or facing your guilt?" asked Fontana. "Watch it. The 'arrangement' or your guilt might swallow you up."

"Let it!" said Cleary, and peeled away from the curb and deeper into Chinatown.

NINETEEN

Johnny cruised up to the curb in his '49 Merc: collar up, elbow out, and feeling totally cool. Sliding out from behind the wheel, he leaned against his hood and faced the Chinese gang kids on their own corner, and claimed a piece of it. A portable radio played Jerry Lee Lewis's "Breathless" at an ear-splitting decibel level, and chicks in skin-tight capri pants, guys in Chinese versions of Elvis haircuts, hung around a '54 chopped De Soto. Of course the Chinese gang flew their green-and-yellow-satin colors instead of white T-shirts and black leather, but that was okay. Variety was the spice of life, or something like that. And everybody had black hair and eyes, but Johnny figured his were just as black. His eyes didn't squint at the corners, and his skin wasn't the color of yellowed piano keys, but what the hell. "Live and let live" was his motto.

He lit a match with his thumbnail, fired up a Lucky, and smiled at the expressions of shock on the kids' faces. He shrugged and took a drag on his cigarette. Facing a gang just depended on having guts, and he had never had any complaints in that department.

A scrawny kid with a neck like a turkey nudged the gang leader. "That's the hillbilly that almost skinned our wheels."

"Oh, yeah?" said the leader, a taller, more muscular kid with the premature lines of leadership etched in his face. He turned to Johnny and played it cool. "Where you want the body sent, man?"

Johnny touched his thumb to his chest. "You talking to me?"

The gang leader took a step closer. "Nobody comes down here on our turf. 'Specially no paddy-faced, redneck white boy."

Waving a finger in mock reproach, Johnny dug back in his memory of infrequent school attendance for the right stiff-assed, disapproving teacher to imitate, and decided on Miss Clements, an old maid history teacher. "Now, now, let's not judge a person by the color of his skin. It is not Christian." He dropped back to his own voice. "So—any of you Chinks know a guy by the name of Tommy Ling?"

Johnny decided that in a contest for the tensest moment of silence, the one following his question had to win the grand prize. The gang stood with their lower lips dragging in the gutter from surprise. Obviously nobody expected the question, or knew how to react to it. Except the leader, who with a *snap-*

click, suddenly held a six-inch switchblade in his hand.

Johnny braced himself. Switchblades. How common. "I came down to help the guy, but if you want to get into it . . ." He opened his coat with a sigh of resignation, and revealed the sawed-off shotgun. "Let's go. I'm ready."

The gang leader was smart enough to know a guy doesn't take a knife to a gunfight, so he stood there studying Johnny. Which was okay by Johnny. He didn't mind as long as the kid came up with the right answer.

"You're crazy, man," the leader finally said. "What makes you think you're getting out of here alive?"

Johnny patted his twelve gauge. "Well, aside from my diplomatic attaché here"—eyes still on the leader, he reached in his car and cranked up his radio, which also blasted out "Breathless"—"we're running on the same dang octane, ain't we?"

Johnny could see that the gang leader was fighting hard, but finally, in spite of himself, he cracked a half smile. All the others followed suit, and the tension evaporated like water spilled on a hot sidewalk. Cautiously Johnny let out his breath. He was glad that was over because he wasn't sure he could've gotten out without ventilating several of the kids. He didn't like the sight of blood; he really didn't.

The gang leader put away his switchblade and shrugged. "No one can help Tommy. He's gonna have to do the time."

"Just why the hell should he do that? He didn't do it."

The same scrawny kid that had alerted the leader to Johnny's presence in the first place spoke up. "Why don't you tell us something we don't already know, man?"

A second kid piped in. "Yeah, like where the guys are from that are pulling off these jobs, man."

The leader shot them a quick look, shutting them up with promises of busted bones if they didn't, but they had already said too much. Johnny considered this new bit of information for a minute, then attempted to keep the conversation alive. Hell, no telling what else turkey-neck might come up with. "Where I come from, guys stand up for each other. We don't let somebody walk up and tell us one of our buddies is going down to the joint, and for us to keep our mouths shut and let it happen. That's a piss-poor stand for a bunch of kids who think they're tough to take."

Several of the gang members bristled at that dig. "Hey, man," said turkey-neck. "You don't know the kind of shit that goes on down here."

"Yeah?" replied Johnny. "You know something? I don't want to know either. It'd just be a bunch of excuses so you won't feel bad when some con in the joint guts Tommy 'cause he don't like Chinks, or just because he had a bellyache that morning."

The leader's eyes narrowed into slits, and he took a menacing step toward Johnny just as a conservative black sedan cruised slowly by. Johnny didn't know who the thin, young man at the wheel was, but he would bet his last dollar that skinny, dried-up man sitting in the backseat who looked as old as God was Uncle Lu. The old man glanced out the window, and seeing Johnny talking to the gang members, leaned over and tapped the driver on the shoulder. The young guy threw a startled look at Johnny, and pulled up to the opposite curb and parked.

Johnny looked around at the gang members and decided he had never seen so many kids whose faces looked like they had just found a cockroach in their egg roll, and decided to pour forty gallons of water down the cook's throat.

Scrawny turkey-neck spoke up again. Evidently he had chronic diarrhea of the mouth, thought Johnny. "We won't have to take this shit for long, man."

"Shut up!" said the leader, renewing his bone-busting promise with his look. He turned to Johnny, his face solemn. "You don't know anything, man." He paused for a measure or two. "If you want to help him, stay out of it."

The gang began to wander off down the street under the watery gaze of Uncle Lu. The leader glanced back, but Johnny couldn't begin to decipher his expression, other than to decide the guy was on simmer, but that it wouldn't take much more heat to bring him to a boil. Johnny wondered how much longer an old geezer like Uncle Lu was going to be able to keep the lid on Chinatown.

The conversation in Chinese between Uncle Lu and the other tong members was subdued, but then Cleary expected that. Certainly Uncle Lu hadn't raised his voice in anger within the living memory of anyone in Chinatown; however, Uncle Lu hadn't needed to. When someone's been as powerful for as long as Uncle Lu, he develops what Betts would call cool. On the other hand, the tong overlord was being challenged for the first time in more years than Cleary was old. Surely that ought to raise the old man's blood pressure at least a little. Unless Uncle Lu thought he had the situation under control by throwing San-Tsiang to the wolves.

He adjusted a dial on his receiver to edit out an occasional squeal from the mike hidden across the street in the herb shop, lifted his headphones a little to ease the pressure on his earlobes, and glanced out the window at the dragon's head of gaudy, flashing neon light on a bar next to the herb shop. He lit a cigarette and let the droning conversation and the impenetrable Chinatown night wash over him. He hated stakeouts. They were always long, boring, and in seedy hotels like this one; the bathrooms were always down the hall and dirty.

He glanced out the window at the mysterious, complex river of faces, silhouettes, storefront gestures, and shadowy transactions, all bathed in the timeless neon glow of Chinatown at night. Between the chatter of singsong Chinese in his ears, and the hypnotic tableau below, his mind drifted back...

...to another restless night when he sat at a table in the back of Frank Tang's bar with Sfakis, Hine, Fontana, and Dibble. The others were relaxed, drinking free booze and bullshitting, at ease with Chinatown, satisfied with the status quo. He was the one who was fighting a sense of loneliness. He watched the cigarette smoke spiral up from the table to add another layer to the already gray-blue haze that swirled lazily, endlessly, toward the ceiling. Frank Tang appeared out of the smoke to deliver another round of drinks on a tray. He passed out the usual to each man, his face a bland, placid mask. With a special flourish, he ran the sliver of lemon peel around the rim of the glass before presenting Cleary with his bourbon and water.

"Thanks, Frank," Cleary said, saluting the Chinese with his glass.

Frank's mask slipped into a half smile. "Always my pleasure, Detective."

No one else at the table even glanced at Tang, and Cleary felt his alienation increase. It was as though he were the only cop who accepted the Chinese as being human. He felt sometimes as though he was suspended between two worlds, his own and that of Chinatown, just as surely as the cigarette smoke hung suspended in midair. But eventually, even the smoke drifted up and dissipated. Only he was in limbo. He pulled his chair closer to the table to listen to the conversation and to feel a part of his world.

"You're way over the line on this one, Cleary," said Dibble.

Cleary took a sip to give himself time to think himself back into the conversation. "If she can't get help from the cops, what are we doing down here?"

Sfakis took a gulp of his drink and sat the glass down with a thud. "We don't want the whole thing to unravel because of one ditzy Chink hooker who thinks she saw something she shouldn't have. Chances are she didn't see a goddamn thing to start with. She just wants to stir things up." .

Cleary shook his head. "Not a Chinese woman. They know their place."

"Maybe she's forgotten," said Hine. "The point is, she's a troublemaker. If we start fooling with this arrangement, the whole thing could come down on us."

Cleary stirred uneasily. He tried not to think of the arrangement, tried to bury his objections in a mass of good reasons why the cops and the tong should work together. "She's a kid who's been through the wringer, and she's scared," he protested.

Dibble looked across the table at him. "You're either on the team or you're not, Cleary. We can't have any one-man grandstanding."

Heads turned toward him, and he felt almost pinned to his chair. This was how a suspect felt getting the third degree.

"You're one of us, Cleary," said Hine, extending a welcome back into their world.

Fontana interrupted, frown lines slashing between his eyes. "Wait a minute," he said. "Don't get the wrong idea, Jack. It's your choice whether or not to pursue this thing. You gotta follow your instincts."

Cleary looked around the circle of faces. These were his friends, his coworkers, part of the world of cops. His world. He raised his glass as...

...a door slammed behind him, and a voice shattered the image from the past. "Hey, Cleary, you asleep, or just checking your eyelids for cracks?"

Johnny Betts strolled across the room, working on an order of Chinese takeout. "I tell you, Uncle Lu and the whole tong could've walked through that door and celebrated Chinese New Year, and you wouldn't have even heard them. Your face looks like you just got out of a matinee. What do you see out of that window that's so damn interesting?"

Cleary took a deep breath. "Nothing. I was just daydreaming."

Johnny gave him a disbelieving look. "Yeah. Well, let me tell you something, boss. Chinatown ain't the place to be caught with your pants down and your mind out the window." He offered Cleary some chow mein, then gestured at the headphones. "Whattya got so far?"

Declining the offer of chow mein, the very smell of which threatened to make him sick, he wearily removed the headphones and rubbed his eyes. "Nothing but five hours of Mandarin. I don't suppose you did any better."

Johnny gave an elaborate shrug. "Depends on how you look at it. You were right about the kid being innocent." He hesitated, his eyes gleaming with an expression Cleary could almost believe was excitement. "According to the Joe Boys, these gambling heists are being pulled by some outside operators."

Cleary straightened out of his slump. "Outsiders?" He saw Johnny's proud nod. "Those gang kids actually *talked* to you?"

Johnny swaggered around the room. "Turns out we belong to the same fraternity"—he grinned—"Sigma Bebop Epsilon A Lula."

"I knew you were good for something, Betts, but I never thought—"

"Hey, they just switched over to AM," Johnny broke in, pointing to the tape recorder.

"W-What?" asked Cleary, trying to follow the conversation.

"They're speakin' English, man. English!"

Cleary jumped up. "Turn it up, damn it! Quick!"

Johnny dived at the tape recorder and gave the knob a vicious twist that made Cleary wince. "That's expensive equipment! Be careful!" he snapped at Johnny, then watched the spools turning as the voice of Uncle Lu filled the small room.

"Yes, the Joe Boys understand. Sacrifices are a necessary part of business."

" 'Sacrifices,' " said Cleary, looking at Johnny. "The Joe Boys must have been forced to make a deal with the tong. . . ."

Johnny nodded, finishing the thought. "So they gave up Tommy. They don't like it either. It got jammed down their throats from what I could tell."

Cleary motioned to silence as Uncle Lu's quivering voice suddenly resumed. "There's no need for that."

There was a long pause during which Cleary realized that he was listening to one end of a phone conversation. The question was: who was on the other end?

"Yes, that's right," continued Uncle Lu's voice. "The association agrees to the new arrangement—providing we have assurances that the violence will end."

There was another long pause, and Cleary spent it wondering how many 'arrangements' the tong had going. There was the arrangement with the police, with the Joe Boys, and now one with whoever was on the other end of that phone line.

"Your word has always been sufficient," said Uncle Lu's voice. "Payment will be delivered tonight at two A.M. by my nephew, Ko-Chen Lu, at the usual place. Good-bye."

A receiver clicked as Uncle Lu hung up, followed by a very short pause, then the old man uttered one word in Chinese. Cleary didn't need a bilingual dictionary to translate. Uncle Lu had obviously used a very dirty word.

"Payment will be delivered tonight at two A.M. by Ko-Chen Lu," said Johnny in a thoughtful tone of voice.

"With you and me tied to his tail, Betts," said Cleary, grabbing his coat and dancing across the room. "We got 'em, kiddo. Somebody just made the old fox blink." In the exuberance of the moment, he forgot himself and tousled Johnny's hair, a gesture he immediately regretted in view of the depth of hair cream on the kid's pompadour. But what the hell, he thought. Live dangerously.

He did a soft-shoe all the way to the door. "Come on, kid. We're through here, and I've got to see somebody before we set up tonight's tail." He turned around to see Johnny Betts trying to smooth his mangled pompadour, and looking at Cleary as if he were personally responsible for running over Lassie.

The first thing Cleary saw was the bolt of scarlet cloth, spilling a bloodred pool of silk across the room. The sewing machines waited in rows, like domestics lined up for the butler's inspection. Other bolts of cloth, their colors appearing washed out compared to the scarlet, were stacked against the walls. The mirrors were smashed into shards, each a sliver of a shattered dream, each reflecting a shattered woman.

Cleary turned around to Kai-Lee. "They got to you."

Her face was a young-old mask; young in years, old in fatalistic resignation. "My dreams were foolish. There's still a place for me though. They said they'd allow me to continue."

"At a sweatshop," Cleary finished. "Just what Chinatown needs."

"You don't understand..."

"I understand you're letting your brother take the fall for a murder rap."

Kai-Lee stood with downcast eyes, the perfect picture of Chinese womanhood. It made Cleary sick. "We'll wait for him to come back to us. An arrangement can be made."

He grabbed her shoulders and shook her until her black silky hair flew about her face. "An arrangement! Goddamn it, there are enough arrangements in Chinatown, and each one of them costs someone's blood. Or someone's dream," he added, looking around at the sewing machines and bolts of cloth. "Maybe that's what makes me so angry about the tong. They're not satisfied with throwing your brother to the wolves; they have to smash your dream, too. All in the name of some kind of perverted arrangement. Listen to me, Kai-Lee. What difference did it make to them if you had a dance studio? Did it cost them money? No! They took away your dream because it was their way of taking away choice. You chose to do something different. The tong can't tolerate that. No free choice in Chinatown. Fight them! Choose to help your brother! I can prove he's innocent."

Her sobs echoed in the room, the mirrors reflected a hundred crying faces. "I'm begging you. Leave us alone. Don't come here again. Leave us alone."

Cleary wanted to push her away in rage and disgust. But he didn't. She had had all the rage one fragile woman could handle. He released her gently and spent his anger on his words. "Turn off the waterworks, baby. Nothing you or the tong or the cops can do will stop me. Not this time. I've got a choice."

He walked out onto the sidewalk and toward his Caddy. His hands were wet and he was breathing too hard, as if he had just gone fifteen rounds. Actually he had. And lost. How long was he going to butt his head against the wall of Chinese fatalism and fear? As long as it took. Until he made a difference.

He yanked open the door of the Eldorado, slid in, and started the black monster, for once not in the mood to admire it's dual-finned beauty. He hit the accelerator, glancing in his rearview mirror as he peeled rubber away from the curb.

"Goddamn it!" Cleary shouted as a black sedan with four men came up fast, the ugly snout of a sawed-off .410 shotgun sticking out of the open rear

window on his side. He threw himself across the fron
seat as the sedan pulled up beside him and the shot
gun exploded into flame.

The shotgun blew a hole through the driver's sea
taking out the entire windshield and showering th
Chinatown sidewalk with glass and upholstery. Th
Cadillac rolled to a stop, and Cleary raised himself o
the front seat.

"Not this time, you damn bastards! Not this time!"

TWENTY

Cleary stretched his arm across the back of Johnny Betts's '54 Merc and tried to relax. He wished he could sleep, but he didn't have time. He and Johnny were parked in the alley across the street from the herb shop. There was no way Ko-Chen Lu could get away without their seeing him. Tonight would be the end of any obscene little arrangement between the tong and the robbers. With any luck, tonight might mark the end of the tong. Once Chinatown knew the tong was weak enough to blackmail, then their power would seep away. There wouldn't be any more dreams wrecked by evil old men.

He watched the hookers, hustlers, and uptown thrill seekers flow past the storefront and the alley

mouth. Uncle Lu and Mickey Gold had a lot in com
mon. They both fed the bored, the perverse, the ge
rich-quick guys, the seekers after a cheap dream
They both fed on the Tao's and the Kai-Lee's. H
didn't know which was really worse, but if he had
choice, he would give the gold ring to Uncle Lu.

"They gonna be able to fix the Caddy?" aske
Johnny, sitting behind the wheel and restlessly pla*
ing with his suicide nob.

"Yeah. For about five hundred bucks. They ble*
out the driver's seat, That's something else Uncle L
owes me for." He tapped Johnny's arm. "There he i
the one just coming out of the herb shop with th
beat-up briefcase."

"Sure don't look like much, does he?" aske
Johnny, watching Ko-Chen Lu climb into a blac
Studebaker parked at the curb. "And he's not ver
bright, or he'd check out the street."

"He's Uncle Lu's nephew. He doesn't think an*
body's stupid enough to mess with him," said Clear
"Hey, you're on," he added as the Studebaker pulle
away from the curb.

Johnny turned the key and the monster engine e*
ploded into life. Cleary flinched. "This is some vehicl
for a tail. A deaf man could hear it coming for a mile

Johnny eased out the clutch and inched the Mer*
up the alley. "You think that pimpmobile you driv
around would be any better? Everybody in China
town knows that car."

"Just drive. And give him plenty of room."

"Hey, man, I was born to do this."

"You weren't born in Chinatown. Let's go. You'r
going to lose him."

With the low growl of dual carbs reverberating i
the alley, Johnny eased past two costumed partygoer

and turned onto the street. "First I gotta give him plenty of room. Then I'm gonna lose him. Make up your mind, Cleary."

Cleary grabbed the armrest. "He's on to us. I can feel it."

Johnny shook his head as he followed the Studebaker through the neon-lit streets. "You been drinkin' too much java, boss. Or eating too many fortune cookies." He glanced at Cleary. "Five bucks says he ain't."

Cleary peered through the windshield and saw the Studebaker's brake lights as it slowed down at a corner to allow a group of drunken partygoers to pass. "Watch him, Betts!" he said, unease building up at how easy it had gone. Too easy.

The Studebaker eased through the swarm and suddenly accelerated away, speeding down the block, leaving the Merc caught behind the partygoers. "Goddamn it, Betts! You owe me five bucks!"

Johnny impatiently gunned the motor, waiting for the road to clear. "We didn't shake on it. Bet's no good unless you shake on it."

Cleary looked through the Chinese swarming around the Merc like multicolored bumblebees, and silently cursed to himself. He cursed even more when it seemed each one of the partygoers slowed down to stare in the car at the two foreign devils. "It's two o'clock in the morning. Why aren't these people home in bed, for Christ's sake?"

"Relax," said Johnny as the last of the Chinese straggled across the street.

"Relax!" said Cleary. "You're losing him!"

"No sweat. He's only got two chances," said Johnny with a sudden popping of the clutch that almost gave Cleary whiplash and laid down ninety feet of rubber and a trail of black smoke as the Merc exploded after the Studebaker.

"Slim," continued Johnny as he expertly double clutched, laying down another patch of rubber. "And none," he finished.

Cleary grabbed the dashboard as the Studebaker's rear lights appeared to be moving backward toward the front end of the Merc. "How are the brakes on this thing?"

"Great," said Johnny, bringing the Merc's gleaming shark-tooth grille an inch from the Stuebaker's rear bumper. "I can stop on a dime."

Cleary braced himself and prayed for survival when he met Ko-Chen Lu's nervous eyes as the Chinese looked in his rearview mirror. He canceled the prayers. He wouldn't give the tong the satisfaction of bashing his head through the windshield.

"How does it feel to be scared, you little bastard?" he yelled out the window.

"He can't hear you, Cleary," said Betts, concentrating on not driving up the other vehicle's tail pipe.

"Ram him, Betts!" he shouted over the Merc's roaring engine. "I bet he can hear that."

Johnny grinned, and Cleary saw his leg flex as he prepared to floorboard the Merc, when a large vegetable truck suddenly pulled out of a side alley right into the Studebaker's path.

"Shit!" yelled Johnny and stood on the brakes.

Ko-Chen Lu swerved wildly, and the Studebaker took out a fire hydrant in an explosion of water and came to a stop against a brick wall. Its hood popped open and steam spewed from the radiator. The startled truck driver took one look and rocketed down the street, leaving a trail of Chinese cabbages and bamboo shoots in its wake. No wise Chinaman got caught between the tong and two Caucasians. Johnny skidded the Merc to a stop next to the wrecked car, and Cleary hoped there was at least five hundred in damages. Turn about and all that.

Jumping from the Merc, Cleary grabbed Ko-Chen Lu and pulled him out through the Studebaker's window, being careful not to be too gentle about it. He slammed him against the Merc's fender, not being too gentle about that, either. "Who you delivering the money to, Ko?"

The Chinese tightened his lips and said nothing, blinking owlishly at Cleary from behind his steel-rimmed glasses.

Cleary picked him up by his lapels and slammed him against the fender again. "Someone's shaking you down"—he slammed him again—"who? Who's got Uncle Lu on the run?"

Ko-Chen shook his head and Johnny sauntered up to Cleary. "Let me give it a whirl." He cracked his knuckles. "I know a few tricks from the Appalachians that'll make the Chinese water torture seem like a Sunday school picnic."

"You'd just wear yourself out on this guy. Uncle Lu's boys are trained from the cradle."

He let go of the Chinese, and Ko straightened his jacket and smiled. "I knew you wouldn't do anything crazy, Cleary."

"No. I'm going to do something I should've done to start with, instead of wasting my time and putting a dent in the fender." He reached through the Studebaker's window and yanked out the briefcase.

"Hey," Ko-Chen yelled, and reached for Cleary, his hands balled into fists.

Johnny jammed him against the car again. "If

there's really a dent in my fender, I'm gonna put a dent in your head."

Ko-Chen ignored him. "You were never known as a thief, Cleary."

"Don't worry. This will get where it belongs, but I'll give you a receipt." He tucked a card in Ko-Chen's shirt pocket. "Here's my number. Tell whoever you were taking this to that if they want their money, give me a call. I'm sure we can come to some kind of 'arrangement.' Let's go, Betts. It stinks like rotten garbage around here."

"Sure thing, boss," said Johnny, stomping on Ko-Chen's instep with his heavy leather boots on his way around the car. The Chinese let out an agonized yip and Johnny grinned at Cleary. "Told you I knew a few tricks."

Cleary climbed the station house steps just behind a couple of uniformed cops hauling in a little gray-haired lady wearing ground-gripper shoes and a lilac dress with a lace collar. She had varicose veins, a sweet face, and mean eyes.

"This is all a mistake, Officer," she said in her placid, old lady's voice.

The night sergeant wearily rolled a booking form into his typewriter. "Yeah. Just like last time, Sadie." He looked up at the arresting officers. "Okay, guys, where'd you find her this time?"

One of the uniforms, a skinny little cop who'd barely made the LAPD height requirement, pushed a shopping bag across the desk. "Planting a bomb in the ladies' room at one of the clubs on the Strip."

The sergeant backed up and pointed at the shopping bag. "Is that the bomb?"

"Yeah," said the skinny cop. "We brought it along as evidence."

"Did the Bomb Squad check it out?" asked the sergeant.

The cop shook his head. "Naw. Sadie said it wasn't armed."

" 'Sadie said it wasn't armed', " repeated the sergeant slowly. He took a deep breath that must have all gone to his head because Cleary never saw a man's face swell up so fast. "You stupid asshole. You don't take the suspect's word that the sun's shining. Now get that shopping bag out of here and go sit in the park until the Bomb Squad can get here."

The skinny cop scurried out of the station holding the shopping bag at arm's length, and the sergeant started the booking process, his eyes filled with the weary resignation of the longtime cop who's seen everything. "You want the corner cell again, Sadie?" he asked.

She smiled her sweet smile that made her eyes look meaner than ever. "Yes, please. And you will remember to call my brother, the bishop?"

Fontana grasped Cleary's arm. "Come on," he said. "Let's go in my office. My stomach's not up to Sadie tonight."

Cleary followed him through the detective division to a small office overflowing with a filing cabinet, a battered desk issued just after World War I, and a couple of wooden chairs with the finish rubbed off the arms and several sets of initials carved in the back. "So who's Sadie?" he asked, straddling one of the chairs and accepting a paper cup full of coffee.

Fontana rubbed his hand through his hair. "She really is the bishop's sister, but she's also been shaking down some of the nightclubs along the Strip. She tells them if they don't ante up with cash for foreign missions, the Lord will not spare them come Judgment Day. The first owner laughed at her until he had a toilet blown through the ladies' room wall land in the middle of his bar. Last year she hit the poker parlors in Pasadena."

"How come she's not in jail?"

Fontana shrugged, the cynical lines around his eyes looking deeper than even the day before. "She's the bishop's sister. She's above suspicion in the jury's eyes. *And* none of the owners of the poker parlors would prosecute. They were afraid if the word got out, every little old lady with a screw loose in L.A. would be throwing dog shit in their customers' cars."

Cleary laughed. "That's what she did?"

Fontana nodded. "Pretty effective, too. I heard receipts were off sixty percent. Now what have you got on the tong?"

Cleary lit a cigarette and crossed his arms on the back of his chair. "The tong has their own Sadie," he began, and ran through his story, watching the incredulous expression on Fontana's face.

"Nice theory, Jack, and it accounts for all the facts, but there's one thing wrong with it. *No one* extorts money from the tong."

"That's what those holdups are all about, Charlie! Somebody's been turning up the heat, and Uncle Lu and his 'merchants' association' finally caved in. They're scared because it's just like the poker parlor owners and Sadie. If the word gets out, every tough around will want a cut of the action, and the tong can't afford that. It'll disrupt their precious order of things."

He ran his hands through his hair and looked at his ex-partner. "We follow the cash and we got the *real* killers, Charlie. It's our choice. We can save that kid, make the tong lose face, maybe deal the 'association' a death blow, and we make a difference in Chinatown."

"And what if something worse takes the place of the tong?"

"What could be worse? And even if it is, at least the people down there will have a choice."

Fontana fiddled with a fountain pen for a few minutes, then looked at Cleary, hope surfacing in his eyes. "Let me know as soon as they call. I'll free up a couple of teams of backup."

Rodan peered over a small lovers' lane rise, hungrily eyeing two lip-locked, oblivious teenagers in a parked Ford convertible.

"Watch it!" whispered Johnny as he camped out on Cleary's reception room couch, telephone at his side, and eyes riveted to a '54 console TV. "Turn around, you idiots. Can't you hear that overgrown canary flapping his wings?"

He sat on the edge of the couch, his pulse accelerating, waiting for one of the lustful teenagers to look up. "Whatta you nuts, Vinnie? You're about to become part of the food chain and you're more interested in swappin' spit in the back of—"

His voice broke off and he scooted closer to the TV as the teenagers suddenly turned to see the huge prehistoric beast looming over them. Johnny leaned back in horror, shoulders hunched in his best streetwise defensive pose, fists ready to pound Rodan's snout if he should happen to fly out of the TV screen.

The phone rang.

Johnny jumped straight up off the couch, grabbing a lamp as a defensive weapon, and wheeled to face

... The window? The door? *The telephone?* "You son of a bitchin' machine! You coulda given me a freakin' cardiac attack!"

He snatched up the receiver. "Yeah. Whatta ya want?"

He set the lamp down as he heard an unfamiliar voice on the other end of the line. It was them, he thought. The masked men, and he didn't mean the Lone Ranger. He cleared his throat and assumed his best businesslike voice. "He's not here. You can talk to me. I'm his associate." He was, too, in a way, when Cleary thought about it.

He listened a few seconds, trying to place the voice and failing. It was muffled. Probably a handkerchief over the receiver. "Division Street Underpass tomorrow night at ten." He grinned and cracked his knuckles. "Lookin' forward to it."

TWENTY-ONE

The mirrors were gone, replaced by institutional brown walls that already looked smudged and dirty. The air smelled of dust and lint, machine oil and humanity, instead of polished floors and the warm-toast scent of little girls. Even the sunlight splashing through the skylight in the ceiling looked washed out. There was no scarlet cloth spilling over the floor today, thought Cleary. No bolts of blues or greens or bright yellows leaning against the wall. Just rows of sewing machines stacked with unsewn garments of black and brown and dun-colored material. Drab ugly clothes in drab ugly colors. Not only had they smashed her studio, they had apparently returned to steal the color from her sweatshop. He pounded his

221

fist against the door frame. "Those bastards," he said aloud.

There was no reply except the quiet ringing of a small bell coming from a tiny coatroom off to one side. He followed the sound to find Kai-Lee, dressed in a colorless tunic and trousers, kneeling in front of a small Buddhist prayer candle and bell. Her neck was bared and vulnerable as she bowed her head in prayer, and again he thought of an executioner's victim. Except an executioner would be swift and merciful. He would not leave her to bleed until all color was gone from her life.

"Damn them," he spat out.

Startled, she turned round, her eyes fearful as a wounded deer who hears the hunter's step. He dropped the gym bag he was carrying, his arms reaching out. "Kai-Lee," he whispered softly. "Oh, God, Kai-Lee."

She rose, unfolding her legs like a graceful young swan, and glided into his arms to rest her head against his chest. He wrapped his arms around her, feeling the fragile body, sensing her fear, and closed his eyes for a minute. Surely they had a minute to rest together.

She raised her head and gently pushed him away, a blush of embarrassment giving her back a little of the color taken from her. "I haven't prayed in years," she said in a low voice, not looking at him.

He cupped her chin and tilted her head back. "Everything you wanted you're going to have. There's nothing wrong with that."

She wrapped her slender fingers around his arm and shook her head. "It's too late for me. They know I came to you."

"Don't talk like that. You're not dead. Your brother

isn't dead. Things will be different, you'll have choices again. There are other places—"

She put her hand over his mouth. "Not for Chinese. You know that better than the others."

He pushed her hand away and grasped her shoulders. "There's no fence around Chinatown, no bars, no armed guards to keep you in. Only the tong telling you there's no other place. That isn't true. You speak English, you are educated. You can go anywhere. Maybe it won't be easy, and maybe some people won't like you, but that's their choice and their problem. It doesn't mean you have to hide in Chinatown like you're some kind of a leper. There's a lot of children who want to dance."

He caressed her shoulders. "I can help you get a new start somewhere."

Her eyes were brighter, and her back straighter, as if life and youth and hope were returning. "My brother is still in jail. I won't leave him and they know that."

Cleary grinned, suddenly feeling as if he had thrown the winning touchdown, kissed the prettiest girl, inherited a million dollars. "Your brother's bail is five grand." He released her and picked up the gym bag. "And there's a little more in there to get started. After tonight, they won't have anything on him. You'll be free, both of you."

He touched her cheek, relishing the soft warmth of her flesh, then turned and walked away.

"I'm not her, Cleary. This money won't bring her back."

A pain ripped through his chest, and he smelled jasmine all of a sudden. He turned around. "I don't know what you're talking about."

She smiled at him, her lower lip trembling just slightly. "Everyone in Chinatown knows that story."

"Then you know I have to do this," he said, holding back the past by strength of will. "Get your things together. I'll be back for you later."

He walked out of the studio and into the street before the scent of jasmine faded.

The Division Street Underpass was a desolate, urban no-man's land, wrapped in silence and smelling of diesel fuel, rotten garbage, and industrial waste. Cleary waited in one of its ominous shadows and listened to the faint scratching of rats, the rattle of discarded paper cups blown by the wind, and his own breathing. The tension of the stakeout had long since dissipated and pure tedium had replaced it, when minutes passed like hours, and men fought to stay awake. He put out his cigarette and checked his watch.

He heard the crunch of gravel and turned as a cigarette butt landed in a shower of sparks at his feet. A figure moved ponderously out of the shadows.

"Put your corsage in the refrigerator, Cleary. Your date's a no-show," said Sfakis, gesturing at the small leather suitcase at Cleary's feet.

Other figures started moving out of hiding until Fontana, Hine, Johnny, and two more plainclothes detectives circled him. Like vultures, he thought suddenly. Gathered around the carrion of his dead hopes.

"An hour and a half crouching in an aqueduct at my age. How come every time I'm around you, Cleary, my lumbago starts acting up?" asked Hine, rubbing his lower back with both hands.

"It happens, Jack," said Fontana sympathetically. "It was a long shot anyway."

Cleary nodded, looking up the tracks toward Chinatown and wondering what happened. "Why, Charlie? Johnny said the voice on the phone was emphatic about the meet. Why didn't they show up?"

Johnny kicked the gravel, spreading it over the train tracks. "Maybe they smelled a setup, Cleary."

"But how?" asked Cleary, looking around at the faces. There was no response, no expression except puzzlement, or disinterest. It was a familiar scenario. He had seen it before in Chinatown: cops standing around discussing why something hadn't worked. But there was something else, something about the people here.

Hine kicked the suitcase and licked his chops. "What does ten grand look like, anyway?" he asked. "I've never seen that much money together in one place."

Sfakis picked up the suitcase, tested the weight, and with two loud clicks, snapped it open. Hine flicked his flashlight on it. "Shit, Cleary," he gasped. "Who you playing games with?"

Sfakis pulled out a handful of cut-up newspaper. "You trying to make up for your loss of pension, Cleary?"

"Where's the money, Jack?" asked Fontana quietly.

Cleary forced his words through taut lips. "Technically it's not the department's money, Charlie, so I didn't need your approval. I gave it to the kid's sister. It'll help with the bail. If there'd been more, I'd have given her that, too."

Sfakis snorted, snapped the suitcase shut, and slapped it playfully into Cleary's stomach. "I don't know about you, but I've had enough fun for one night. My shift's been over for two hours. Come on,

Hine. I get hungry just coming down here. Let's grab some chow mein."

"Another half hour, Jack. That's all I can give you," said Fontana.

Cleary didn't hear him. He watched Hine and Sfakis crunch away over the gravel, side by side like dissimilar twins, two cops, so familiar to Chinatown, no one ever noticed them. Yet they were always the first on the scene in Chinatown...

... "You got enough?" Hine asked the photographer.

"A couple more," replied the photographer as he lowered his bulky camera and quickly sniffed nasal spray up his nose. Like Hine and Sfakis, he was totally disinterested in this dead Chinese hooker in the scarlet dress.

"I get hungry just coming down here. Come on, Cleary, we're going to grab some chow mein," said Hine as...

...Cleary turned to Johnny, a sense of urgency making him brusque. "Stay with the stakeout."

"Hey, where you going, man?" asked Johnny.

"The masked men. They're just like Sadie. Above suspicion."

"Who the hell is this Sadie?" Johnny asked Fontana as Cleary ran up the tracks toward Chinatown.

TWENTY-TWO

Cleary pushed his way through the madness of a Chinatown parade, a celebration that jammed the streets with laughing, drunken Chinese. Another block to Kai-Lee's studio, another eternity of shoving the seething, dancing, singing humanity aside to take a step. In the cacophony of Chinese music, huge brightly colored dragons, emerald green and fire-engine red, swirled and dipped to an exotic, Oriental rhythm. The air was filled with pieces of paper, like a snowstorm of confetti, emanating from the exploding balls tied on high poles. Firecrackers burst in endless strings of popping noises, showering bystanders with sparks. The crowds on the sidewalks flowed into the street in waves of masked and costumed celebrants.

Cleary pushed harder, slipped by a weaving Chinese in a tall mask, ducked under the head of a dragon and gained the curb. A half block to go, one more street to cross. Blessing his height, he peered over the heads of the shorter Chinese and saw her. She was seated on a suitcase in the dark, recessed entrance to her studio. Relief made him almost lightheaded. She was leaving Chinatown, had in a sense already left it, because she sat quietly, staring out at the passing festival but taking no part in it. She was breaking her bonds one by one.

"Kai-Lee!" he yelled as he saw a man in a mask grab her. He saw her mouth open in a scream, saw her yank the mask off, then sink back against the door, limp-looking from relief. The man, a middle-aged Chinese, drunk and happy, laughed and slapped his knee at her reaction. Still grinning happily, he joined the parade, leaving her slumped in the entranceway.

Cleary blinked away the sweat that ran down in his eyes and took several deep breaths to calm his pounding heart. Maybe he was wrong in his suspicions. It wouldn't be the first time. Maybe he was going off half-cocked. Maybe he was too tired, too depressed, too guilty to think straight. And maybe he was doubting himself because that was the easier choice. Just like the last time.

He waved both arms above his head to catch her attention as he saw her peer our from her entranceway past the flowing river of celebrants. A paper dragon, the fire-engine red one he noticed, passed in front of him, cutting off his view of the studio.

Cleary fought his way through the crowds, using shoulders and elbows to brutally force the celebrants aside. The old, familiar dread was tightening his chest, quickening his step as he outran the dragon and looked directly across the street to Kai-Lee's studio. "Oh, God!" he screamed as he saw two clowns in round, odd, happy-scary Chinese masks suddenly veer away from the parade, grab Kai-Lee and her suitcases, and disappear into her darkened storefront studio.

"No!" he roared, and ducking his head, ripped through the crowds thronging the street. Temporarily blocked by a mother holding a little girl by the hand, he looked up and saw the two clowns viciously beating Kai-Lee in a perverse parody of a comic routine.

Suddenly stooping, he picked up the mother and her child and set them behind him. Turning back around, he gained several feet by knocking down two drunken laborers who smelled of fish. Glancing quickly at the studio windows, he saw Kai-Lee holding on to her briefcase for dear life, using it as a shield against the worst blows. Backing up toward the wall, Cleary saw her grab a knitting needle off one of the sewing machines, and raising her arm, wildly stab one of the assailants.

"You bastard! I'll kill you!" screamed Cleary as the other clown clubbed her with his gun, knocking her to her knees, then grabbed her long black hair to hold her head still, pointing his gun at her temple.

With a final, desperate rush that left at least one Chinese trampled on the sidewalk, Cleary crashed through the front window. Falling on the floor in a shower of glass, he saw the two clowns grab the bag of money and run up the stairs to the roof.

Crawling over to Kai-Lee's body, he reached out to touch her, the scent of jasmine overpowering him, sending him reeling back into his worst Chinatown nightmare. "I tried," he said softly, and not to the girl lying so still on the floor. "I tried this time. But I couldn't stop them."

The scent of jasmine faded as a shadow crossed in front of him on the floor. The two clowns on the roof raced past the neon sign and cast a shadow through the skylight onto the floor. Cleary looked up and threw himself to one side as the clown with a sawed-off shotgun fired through the skylight and blasted a hole in the floor where he was standing.

With a rapid movement Cleary thought he was too beat to make, he turned and fired, bringing the clown with the sawed-off shotgun crashing through the remaining shards of glass in the skylight to fall dead at his feet. Ripping the mask off, Cleary saw the face of Sfakis.

"Why?" he whispered, frozen for a moment with grief for the old, good times. "Why did you do it?"

Shaking off his paralysis, he raced for the stairs. Sfakis couldn't answer his question, but there was one who could. Barreling out of the door, he saw the clown just ahead and chased him across the rooftops. Through antennas, pigeon coops, the guts of neon signs, exhaust pipes spilling out steam, and vents pumping out noxious fumes, he ran, the clown always just ahead. Around him was the neon and chaos and night of Chinatown.

"Hine!" bellowed Cleary, stopping and bracing himself, gun hanging loosely in one hand.

The clown stopped and turned around to face Cleary. Ripping off his mask and dropping it, Hine managed an ugly smile. "Fucking mask. It gets hot under these things."

Cleary faced Hine, saw the gun in his hand, and felt resigned. Below him, he could hear the melee of the street celebration going on. It was fitting, he thought. He had come to slay a dragon, and that called for a celebration.

"Did you know that in Chinese mythology, the dragon is not a symbol of evil, Hine?" he asked.

"What are you talking about, Cleary?"

"In our European fairy tales, the dragon is evil. If I'd remembered that, maybe I'd have dropped on you and Sfakis sooner. I should've looked for a Caucasian dragon, not a Chinese one. It's all very simple when you understand it."

"You're fucking crazy. You've been crazy since that hooker got in the way and had to be killed."

Cleary smelled jasmine. "It was you and Sfakis, wasn't it?"

Hine shrugged. "We were just starting out. It was before we learned that shaking down the tong was easier than holding up restaurants. Shit, Cleary, we never thought you'd go nuts over a Chink hooker."

He sounded almost apologetic, as if he and Sfakis had accidently run over a pet of his, and Cleary surrendered to his rage. "You're going to die like you lived, Hine."

Hine laughed. "That's right, Cleary. With a lake house at Arrowhead, a Lincoln in the garage, and six years of Chink pussy and booze under my belt." He laughed again, looking with disgust at Cleary's dishevelled appearance. "And how's your life been, Boy Scout?"

"It's looking up," said Cleary.

Hine made the first move, raising his gun. Cleary brought his up and began firing. A bullet from Hine's .38 ripped through his left shoulder, numbing it to the wrist, but he kept firing, hitting Hine in the chest, throwing him backward. Hine landed in a sitting position on the very edge of the low wall surrounding the rooftop.

"Not yet, Cleary," he said with a bloody smile, and raised his gun again.

Cleary fired his last round, hitting Hine square in the chest again, throwing him backward off the rooftop. The briefcase opened, and the money flew out like green confetti, filling the air, raining down on the parade below.

Cleary staggered to the edge, blood running down his shoulder, soaking his shirt, and dripping onto the roof. He saw Hine's body, crumpled on the ground, the parade detouring around it, and the money showering down to cover it. He holstered his gun, wincing with pain as he touched his shoulder, and turned back to the stairwell, back to Kai-Lee.

Passing the ancient raised skylight, he saw her lying motionless on the floor of the studio below, a sewing machine throwing a grotesque shadow over her body. He stared at her lifeless form. "No," he whispered as the scene wavered...

...becoming a street of Chinatown in front of a restaurant. Bodies lay on the sidewalk, some motionless in death, others moaning and writhing as the pain from gunshot wounds burned through them. Police cars were parked angled toward the curb, their headlights serving as spots for the crime scene. Ambulances pulled up in a stream to help the living, take away the dead. Cops stood around in the inevitable circle: Dibble, Hine, Sfakis, Fontana—and Cleary.

A beautiful Chinese hooker in a scarlet dress slipped out of the crowd and walked hesitantly toward Cleary. He saw her motioning, and he dropped out of the circle. He noticed her pale face and wide frightened eyes. She ought to be frightened, he thought.

She was breaking all the taboos of Chinatown by talking to a cop.

"Please," she said, clutching at his arm.

"You got anything for us? Someone must have seen something. Nobody could shoot up a place as badly as this and do it without being seen," said Cleary, lighting a cigarette.

"Will you help me?" the hooker whispered, her eyes veering toward the circle of cops behind him.

Cleary took a drag off his cigarette, and deliberated. "That depends," he said, studying her face...

..."I'm sorry," he whispered as the street dissolved into the rooftop and the ancient skylight. The scent of jasmine grew stronger.

Escaping from the roof, he rushed down the stairs and fell to his knees besides Kai-Lee's prone, lifeless body. "I'm sorry," he said, his voice hoarse and thick with guilt.

Taking her in his arms, the scent of jasmine became overpowering. "I can't do anything," he cried to the past, then instinctively, urged by something he couldn't explain, he checked Kai-Lee's carotid pulse. "You're alive," he said, clutching her tighter, watching her eyes beginning to flutter open.

"An ambulance is on the way," a voice said.

Cleary looked up to see Frank Tang standing over him, studying him. "Thanks," he said, and turned back to Kai-Lee, brushing her hair away from her face, cushioning her brutalized body against his chest.

Feeling Frank Tang's eyes still on him, he glanced up again. "I thought I could make a difference this time."

Frank Tang nodded, a faint smile twisting his lips

and casting its shadow in his eyes. "This time you did."

Cleary nodded, and looked down at Kai-Lee again. The scent of jasmine was gone, and its absence felt permanent.